CLAIMED BY THE FOX CAPTAIN

SCIFI ALIEN MM ROMANCE

FURRY ALIEN MATES
BOOK 2

DELANEY RAIN

CLAIMED BY THE FOX CAPTAIN © 2024 by Delaney Rain

All rights reserved.

No part of this book may be reproduced in any form or by any electronic or mechanical means, including information storage and retrieval systems, without written permission from the author, except for the use of brief quotations in a book review.

Cover design by Delaney Rain Author Services. Any person depicted on the cover is a model.

Formatting by Delaney Rain Author Services

NO AI/NO BOT. I do not consent to any Artificial Intelligence (AI), generative AI, large language model, machine learning, chatbot, or other automated analysis, generative process, or replication program to reproduce, mimic, remix, summarize, or otherwise replicate any part of this creative work, via any means: print, graphic, sculpture, multimedia, audio, or other medium. I support the right of humans to control their artistic works.

Knot Icon by Kick from The Noun Project (CC BY 3.0)

With thanks to Tammy, Nicole, and Trace for their collective advice and eagle eyes.

*For all of the members of the
Queer Monster Romance Sanctuary Facebook Group.*

GLOSSARY

These are the races of Norlons as they refer to themselves and how humans interpret those names:
- Pip = anthropomorphic rabbits
- Yook = anthro wolves
- Khess = anthro felines
- Cero = anthro lizards
- Beku = anthro otters
- Lago = anthro foxes

CHAPTER 1
CAPTAIN PYSINA LANGARUS

I blinked at the ceiling, my heartbeat and breaths loud in my ears. Why was everything red? Then it was as if my ears popped because I could suddenly hear far too much. Klaxons wailed, the blaring alarms beating out every other sound and making me tuck my ears down to try and escape the hideous noise. And that was when I remembered what had happened.

A bomb. One of the humans had detonated a bomb strapped to himself. He'd screamed something about Humans First and then tried to kill us all.

As captain, I wasn't able to escape any of this. I was in charge.

My back protested as I sat up, a sharp pain shooting down to my left knee, but it was the human who slumped from against my chest down to my lap that truly concerned me. *Friend or foe?* But since the lean young man was unconscious, his intentions didn't matter much at the moment.

I cupped the back of the man's head and felt for a pulse at his neck. Strong and steady. Maybe the explosion had thrown him into me and knocked him out. He didn't smell like a threat—he actually had a very pleasant scent. Reassured for now, and needing to engage with the recovery efforts, I held the man close to my chest and stood up.

A quick look around showed me security and medical personnel rushing in and doing their assessments. Commander Sorke sprinted toward me, and I pulled him closer when I couldn't hear a single thing the Lago said.

"Shut these damned alarms off!" I nearly screamed into Sorke's round ear.

Sorke nodded and ran off, leaving me to hope he knew where the controls were. I knew my ship but not every button and switch. Blessedly, it was just seconds before the klaxons quit their screeching.

But in the quiet, now I could hear the cries and moans of the injured and dying. My heart constricted in horror and sympathy as the security personnel and my own commanders gathered around me, awaiting their orders.

"Security, support the medics. Have them triage everyone in the cargo hold. Open the doors completely so there's easier access." They rushed off as a horrible thought occurred to me. "The royals! Has anyone seen—"

"There, sir," Sorke said beside me, and I followed his pointed finger to where Prince Ye Lena and his new prince-consort were standing. I took a steadying breath and refocused.

"I need every human checked for weapons, even the bodies. And get me a damage report. Are the bay doors holding?" I looked to the damn things, willing them to hold even as I saw some part of a shuttle embedded in one side like a knife.

"Engineering is on the way," Lieutenant Commander

Rigger, a tall gray Yook, said before he too cast a worried glance at the doors.

I nodded at that. "Someone get on the bay's main control panel and keep an eye on the atmosphere in here. I want to know if there's even the slightest loss of pressure."

"Yes, sir," Rigger said before jogging away.

"Once the bay is clear, we seal it off as if there's been a breach. I want no chances taken here."

"Yes, sir," the rest of them said.

"Go!" I barked when they didn't move. "Check the humans and get that damage report."

They scattered, but at least they looked like they knew where they were going. As I watched them go, I saw Seiwa Heremod jet around the room like his fuzzy white tail was on fire. As head engineer, this had to be one of his nightmares, but he was calm and focused even as he leapt from place to place near the shuttle.

As I watched him, I realized there was a hole in the flooring. Thank the goddess the explosion had gone down into another cargo hold instead of up into crew quarters—third shift would've been in their bunks at this hour.

"Sir?" a Lago medic said as he approached me. "Is he alive?"

I blinked at him in confusion. "Who?"

"The human you're holding."

I looked down, alarmed and even more confused to find that I still held the skinny man against my chest, one arm looped under his and hugging him tightly to me. I hadn't noticed. I hadn't meant to carry him with me.

"I… Yes, he's alive. Just…unconscious."

The medic was nodding as he approached like I might fight him off. "Can I take him? I'll evaluate him right here."

Why was my first instinct to turn away and deny him

access? That didn't make any sense. A medic wanted to help an injured person. I shouldn't prevent that.

"Of course," I said and stepped closer to the medic. "You can take him."

He did and eyed me cautiously while he eased the human into his arms and laid him on the floor at our feet. There were things I needed to do, but I stood there watching the medic evaluating the human instead. I couldn't make myself look away.

"He has a severe concussion," the medic said up to me. "Should I treat him now, or wait for him to be conscious enough to consent?"

He shouldn't have even asked me, and I knew what I should do, but I didn't hesitate to say the opposite. "Do it now."

The medic nodded and prepared a syringe. I couldn't stop the growl that left me when he stuck it into the man.

"I apologize," I said when the medic looked up at me.

"It's alright, sir. I understand."

Did he? Why didn't I?

"Now let's see to you." The medic stood and moved around behind me.

"There's nothing wrong with me." Except for the fact that I needed to pick the human up again and was trying to resist that urge.

"You're bleeding, sir."

I followed his pointing finger to see a small pool of blood under my left boot. "Fuck," I said as the pain suddenly registered. I made to reach back, touch where it hurt, but the medic grabbed my wrist to stop me.

"There's a piece of something embedded in your lower back. Just be still for me." He let my wrist go and came around in front of me again, scanning me with one of his devices like he'd done with the human at my feet. "I need a gurney!" he yelled over his shoulder.

"I can walk," I protested, but the instant I tried to, my left knee buckled like it wasn't even connected to the rest of my body.

The medic caught me under my arms, and I couldn't help the yelp that left my throat as the sudden move pulled at whatever was stabbing into me. I wanted to reach back and rip it out of me, but even the pain didn't let me forget how badly I might bleed if I did.

A moment later and two more medics arrived with gurneys, the three of them settling me on one and the human on the other.

"Keep them together," my medic told everyone.

I wasn't sure if I wanted to ask what he knew as I kept my gaze on the unconscious young man being pushed down the corridor beside me.

CHAPTER 2
OWEN DEVIN

I woke up slowly, blinking a lot under bright lights that dimmed a moment later. The wall over my head was covered in symbols and words I couldn't read, lights flashing and… It was medical information because that red dot was pulsing with my heartbeat and that line lifted up every time I took a breath.

Oh fuck. Oh god. I was in an alien hospital. On a space ship. Because my…my fucking father was a lunatic bomber piece of shit who'd tried to kill us all! A sob ripped out of me and I covered my mouth as I tried to fight back the horror inside me.

"Easy," a low voice said beside me. "You're alright."

Gasping, I looked to my right and found a giant fox staring at me. I knew what his type was really called, but nope, I couldn't remember it right now. Something that started with an L? Whatever. His sort of golden orange eyes gazed at me steadily as he laid on his side facing me. Someone who looked like a huge snow leopard was behind the fox and… Shit, were they performing surgery? While the fox was awake?

"I'm fine," the fox said. "Don't worry about me."

I swallowed hard and couldn't resist saying, "I thought you guys used nanobots for everything." I knew they had nanobots that could heal all kinds of things, but the fact that the leopard behind him was making moves like they were stitching him up was alarming.

"There was a piece of debris in my back," the fox said oh-so-calmly. "While the nurse stitches me closed, the nanobots are working on repairs on the inside. How's your head?"

"Fine?" I reached up and touched my head, sifting through short black curls like there might be something to find. "Why?"

"You had a severe concussion. I approved the medic's use of nanobots on you."

The leopard nurse stitching him up paused to look between us, and I thought maybe I knew why.

"Without my permission?"

He looked me right in the eyes and said, "I couldn't let you to suffer."

I lay back and stared up at the ceiling. Did that bother me? These people had pumped me full of microscopic robots to treat a severe concussion—and I'd never had a regular one, so I didn't know what severe really meant. I knew from their website what the nanobots would do inside me, that I'd pee them out when they were done, and that they were safe for me as a human.

I probably wasn't the only one who'd gotten this up close and personal demonstration thanks to my fucking father's actions either.

"Thank you," I said as I looked back at the fox.

The corner of his black lips curled up in an almost-smile.

"Did, um… Did anyone die?" I finished that question breathlessly, horrified all over again.

"Eight have died," he said.

I nodded and looked away, closing my eyes as tears threatened. How the hell had I missed the fact that Dad had covered himself with explosives? How had I not known that he was a Humans First sympathizer? We weren't that close anymore, but I hadn't had a clue that he wanted to kill people.

Had he let me come with him so he could kill me, too?

Suddenly, a tone sounded, making me flinch. I looked up at the readings on the wall over my head, but nothing looked like a problem. What was happening? Then a voice sounded as if over a loudspeaker.

"This is Prince Alam Ye Lena speaking on behalf of the delegation to thank each of you for your swift actions and professional dedication as we work through this painful time. While we mourn and repair, know that the humans of Earth are protesting the faction that hurt us and demanding their leaders take steps to condemn it. Though their enlightenment has come at a heavy price, I believe now that they see us for what we are: a people who are determined to raise them up to our level of comfort and safety. I have not changed my course, and I hope you have not either." He paused for a moment before continuing. "Seek out and accept assistance where and when you need it as you move through your grief. We are all here for you."

The tone sounded again, and my tears fell.

Good god, how could anyone be against these people? They might be skirting around the governments of the world, but it was to aid all of humanity regardless of how we kept getting in their way. They were doing everything legally, too —I'd seen some of the paperwork from their *human* lawyers. But still, if someone was offering you a helping hand, you didn't ask them if they had a permit first! How could my own father be such a fucking terrorist?

"Sir!"

I snapped my attention to the fox and saw that he was attempting to get up off the gurney.

"Sir, I'm not done yet," the leopard said as she tried to hold him down. "You can't get up!"

The fox stared into my eyes, and I didn't know what else to do but meet his golden gaze. Eventually, he settled back down, and the leopard waved off the pair of wolves who had been coming over like security. She rearranged a sheet over the fox, but not so well that he was covered up completely.

I couldn't help staring. While he was lean, he was pretty ripped. Even his black, orange, and cream fur couldn't hide the definition of his arms and abs. And I knew about the relationship that wolf prince had with a human cop, so I was allowed to appreciate that this fox was hot, right? They were all just furry people after all.

But then I realized he'd caught me staring and I looked away before mopping up my tears with the cuff of my sleeve. I wasn't in any kind of position to flirt and didn't deserve the attention anyway.

"What's your name?" the fox asked.

"Owen D—" I stopped myself from admitting my family name when before I would've been proud of that. But never again.

Never again.

"I'm Py. Pysina Langarus."

I nodded and tried to offer him a smile even as my eyes burned with more tears I didn't want to shed. Then I remembered— "Oh, you're the captain."

And why knowing that kicked off another round of

sobbing, I didn't know. Because it was probably his subordinates who'd died? Yeah, fuck, that was part of it, but also I felt so responsible. I'd urged my father to accept the invitation to come here in the hope that seeing would make him stop hating.

"Sir!" I heard the nurse holler just before furry arms lifted my upper body from the gurney and hugged me close against a strong chest. Captain Langarus should hate me, but instead he was risking injury to hold me while I cried. I didn't deserve any such attention, but I buried my weeping face between his pecs, curled my hands on his abs, and let it all out.

I didn't know how long I leaned on him and wept over the lives lost, my own circumstances, and my father's betrayal, but eventually I realized Langarus was having a conversation with someone.

"Commander Heremod said the damage to the landing bay is extensive," a quiet and deep voice said, "but not life-threatening. The hull is unaffected and not likely to become compromised. However, he's fine with continuing to treat the area as though there's been a breach, if you prefer."

"It's his call," Langarus said just as quietly. "Did you search the other humans?"

I sniffed, and he petted my hair.

"We did. All of them except…"

"They checked him here. He's clear."

Oh, that was about me. Someone must've searched me while I was out. Of course they should've. I was probably a suspect. On the terror watch list. I'd never be allowed to fly again. Passport revoked. And a part of me felt I deserved all of that for how utterly ignorant I'd been.

"Excuse me, Captain," someone else said in a low voice.

"Thank you. Set it all there," Langarus said, and I felt

something soft rest against my hip. I didn't want to look and have to meet the eyes of anyone nearby despite being curious about what they'd brought him.

"Does Seiwa have an estimate for when we can use the bay again?" Langarus asked, making me realize we were probably surrounded by people needing him to lead them. Part of me wanted to slink away and let him do his job. The rest of me couldn't stop clinging.

"Commander Heremod said the floor is too compromised to handle the weight of the shuttles," that same low voice said, "so he's had all of the working ones moved to docking collars throughout the ship."

"When you're finished questioning the humans," Langarus said without even a hint of malice, "get them back to the surface."

I leaned a little more against him. How pathetic was I that I didn't want to go home? Hiding up here sounded way better than going down there where the press would probably destroy me. Because they had to know something had happened even if no one had told them what yet since that PBS News crew had been with us the whole time. No reporter anywhere in the world would ignore an explosion.

"Well, sir, we mentioned that and… Sir, they don't want to leave."

"What?"

They didn't either? Made sense to me, but I wasn't a political leader who could milk this for more votes and donations. What was their reasoning?

"They want to continue on with the scheduled events. It's like they're even more determined to learn and change minds, sir. I hate to say it, but—"

"The terrorist had the opposite effect than what he'd wanted."

Well, that got me looking up in surprise.

He petted a hand over my cheek, and there was so much more than just offering comfort in his beautiful golden eyes. Nothing else should be there—hell, comfort shouldn't be there—but I got the feeling he wanted me naked and alone with him. I swallowed hard, staring, and totally unsure if I would say no to such a suggestion if he asked.

Someone cleared their throat, and Langarus blinked a few times like he was coming out of a daze. I could relate.

"Tell them that we need some time to reset, but that we appreciate their dedication."

Langarus reached for that thing beside me, and I realized it was his uniform. Or a fresh one since they'd probably had to remove the old one to stitch him up. It was as he started dressing that I realized he was naked.

Even as lost as I felt, I was still disappointed that I couldn't see much through the cream-colored fur at his groin. A hint of a sheath for his cock and a tease of a sac below that was all I saw before he pulled up a pair of black slacks that hugged his contours beautifully.

"For the humans on the list," Langarus said as he buttoned up his red tunic-like coat, "assign a monitor to them. In fact, give all of them a wristband."

He paused and gazed down at me, looking every bit as official and intimidating as he had when I'd stepped off the shuttle in the landing bay. Right then, I remembered seeking him out when I'd realized what my father had strapped to his chest. Of course I'd gone for the strongest person in the room when I'd been so terrified.

"We're aware that some of the human visitors were against

us," Langarus said to me. "We invited them for that reason. Obviously, we were unaware of how severe the governor's leanings were."

"I'm sorry," I whispered.

He nodded. "You're going to be accompanied by someone everywhere you go and will wear a device that can monitor your exact location and physical responses, like your pulse. Yes, it's designed for prisoners—"

"It's okay. I deserve it."

"Do you?"

"I had no idea he could do something so *evil*." I gulped back more tears and looked down at my hands in my lap. "Do whatever you want with me."

I felt his hand touch the back of my neck and the subtle scratch of his claws as he gripped me there. I stayed still and let him.

CHAPTER 3
PYSINA

Everything in me wanted to mark little Owen as mine. Dear goddess, what was happening to me? Never in my life had I been so urged to claim someone. The circumstances of this moment were completely wrong for such desires, and yet if he twitched at all, I might mate him right there in the infirmary before my commanders and the entire medical staff—including the Khess who wanted to skin me for not letting her properly dress my wound.

But Owen held still under my hand, not even reacting to the touch of my claws on his delicate flesh. Head bowed, neck bared, he waited. Could he truly mean to allow me to do whatever I wished with him?

"You'll bunk with me," I told him as I made myself withdraw my hand. I clenched it into a fist when I realized it was shaking.

Owen nodded without looking up at all.

My commanders stared at me in surprise. Commander Sorke, a fellow Lago, took a step back as he nodded at me.

Not at all ready to declare what was truly pulsing through me, I gave a reason that they might accept. "He's the governor's son. I want to keep him close," I explained and watched their expressions change as they frowned at him. But I also didn't want them hating him and couldn't stop my snarl.

All three of them snapped their attention back to me. Maybe Owen deserved closer observation, like some of the others, but after holding him while he wept, I doubted he was a threat to anyone but himself.

"Captain," Lieutenant Commander Rigger said, "we've determined that two others were also part of the governor's people and are among the humans killed."

Owen made a whimpering sort of noise and hunched lower over his knees. I couldn't resist putting my hand back on his neck again, this time in comfort.

"Is the prince aware of the humans' intention to remain?"

"Yes, sir," Commander Evish said, and I realized the Pip's hand was bandaged.

"Are you alright?" I asked her with a nod at her hand.

She waved my concerns away. "Oh, yes, sir. It's just a cut."

Like with my injury, the nanobots would work from the inside while medication and wrappings were needed on the outside. The both of us should be fine by evening.

"Where are the humans now?" I asked the three of them as I wondered if I could leave Owen with them while I saw to everything that needed my attention.

Rigger answered. "The large conference room. We're working on housing them in group bunks so that they can remain with their individual parties."

"Sir," Evish said, "the news crew has asked that they be allowed to film the recovery efforts and interview crew members such as yourself and Commander Heremod."

She'd mentioned something similar before Owen woke. "To add to what they've broadcast to the surface already?"

"Yes, sir."

I nodded but wasn't ready to commit to any such thing. "Talk to the delegation. I'd prefer they lead the conversation for now."

"Yes, sir."

When no one else offered anything, I said, "Have someone from Security who's prepared to take first watch meet me at my cabin with a tracker. I'll be on the bridge within the hour."

They took their leave, and I turned my attention to Owen. "Do you feel well enough to walk?" I asked him.

He nodded, his posture looking as though he was trying to collapse in on himself. I had to step back so that he could slip off the gurney and stand in front of me. The top of his head came to my collarbones, and all I wanted to do was clutch him to my chest.

Lightly gripping the back of his neck seemed to quell my urges and I used that grip to walk him toward the exit. On the way, I spotted Doctor Revazi and paused to query him on the injured.

"Everyone's responding nicely to the nanobots," he said with a small and tired smile. His normally jovial face looked haggard as even his long Beku whiskers were drooping.

"None of the visiting humans protested?" I'd been in on the preparations for this entire event and had known some—like the deceased governor—would likely balk at most of our demonstrations.

"Not one resisted. We had several questions, but nothing unusual, and all who needed them consented to their use."

I watched Revazi's large yellow eyes glance at Owen, but I wasn't going to explain myself a second time.

"Is everyone recovering?" I asked instead.

Revazi sighed heavily. "All but one. A Petty Officer Digish

has been badly burned in the center of his back. As a Cero… Well…" He tried to smile. "We're going to keep trying."

I knew what he didn't want to say. Ceros had scaly hides that could resist a wide range of penetrative injuries, but fire was particularly horrible for them. Their scales could trap flame and heat against their flesh, making burns tunnel into them, destroying muscle and sometimes even bone. While they could regrow severed limbs, that the burn was center mass and on the petty officer's back might mean that the nanobots and submersion therapies wouldn't be enough to stop the devastation if it reached his spine.

"Please keep me informed of their progress," I said and mentally tried to prepare for the worst. "Is there anything else I need to know?"

Revazi glanced at Owen again, making me realize that we both spoke English as if to include him. It would've been far more normal for us to speak Norlish, but it seemed I was already conditioning myself to make sure Owen understood me always. I'd even spoken English with my commanders.

"Nothing that can't wait for my daily report," Revazi said. "I'll include the petty officer's progress in there."

I reached out with my free hand to grip Revazi's shoulder. "I know I don't need to tell you this, but I'm going to say it anyway. Let me know if you need anything, and don't hesitate to step back if you need the time away. That goes for your entire team as well."

For a brief moment, I could see the toll the day had taken on him. While space missions were all inherently dangerous, neither of us had anticipated such conflict with this one. We'd seen enough of the horrors of war twenty years ago when we had defended our world from the Vigzek, an elitist people who had wished to enslave Norlons much the same as they had been doing to the humans of Earth that they had abducted.

Revazi nodded and said, "Thank you. I'm going to check in with everyone now and see where we stand."

"And take care of your—"

Revazi smiled and patted my side. "And take care of myself as well. You should heed your own advice, Py."

I nodded and gave his shoulder a squeeze before steering Owen around him and out the door. Neither of us was going to take our own advice. I knew I should, but I had too much to do. There was no possible way I could excuse myself for a break. Revazi probably wouldn't—

"That was nice of you," Owen whispered once we were in a lift.

"Pardon?"

I felt him gulp. "I just mean, it's nice that you care. About his mental health and all. Most leaders I've known…" He shrugged, staring at the floor. "They don't seem to care if someone's struggling."

"Then they aren't leaders."

Owen looked up at me, clearly startled. I met his gaze, standing behind what I'd said. No one could call themselves a leader of others if they didn't take into account whether those working for them were healthy. Revazi and I had past experience to help us through these events, but plenty of others may have never known such traumas. Prince Ye Lena had it right that counseling services would be needed by many.

"Yeah," Owen whispered, "I guess they're not."

The lift doors opened onto the deck with officers' quarters, and I was glad to see that an ensign was waiting outside my door. The Khess held a tracker in her hands and watched Owen closely as we approached. I didn't mind the scrutiny since it would be another set of eyes on him for his protection.

Who or what was I protecting him from? I didn't know.

The ensign fitted the tracker to Owen's right wrist, the lightweight band hugging his every contour like a second skin. She said there would be a four-hour rotating watch of security personnel at the door before she took her leave to stand at her post. Owen and I were alone for the first time.

I still wanted to ravish him, but instead of it being something I could barely contain, it simmered inside me. Could it have been that I needed him marked as mine when others were near?

Goddess, did I truly need to speak with a mated Lago to find out if that was what plagued me? I remembered the medic who had initially treated me in the landing bay and tried to remember his name. He'd recognized something in my behavior, so perhaps—

"Could I contact some people?" Owen asked quietly.

Snapping myself out of my own issues, I nodded and gestured to the monitor on the wall. "Of course you can. Let me alert the switchboard to your presence here, and they can help you reach anyone on Earth."

"I'm sure everyone…knows if the news crew kept filming and all, but I should probably still check in with…someone."

Before I activated the monitor, I looked him in the eyes. "Because of your situation, all communication will be monitored."

He gulped visibly and nodded. "I understand. I'm just going to let them know I'm not…dead and confirm… I mean, they probably saw it all, but I want to make sure…" He sighed heavily and looked away. "I'll make sure they know he really did do it. I don't want to let them cover it up or spin it somehow."

"Spin it?" I asked as I tapped out a message to the switchboard operators in Communications with my authorization.

"Make it into something it's not," he said bitterly. "Say something stupid, like he had an allergic reaction and didn't know what he was doing."

"He knew."

"Yeah."

I pointed at the monitor. "When you're ready, tap this blue icon, and someone will help you make contact."

He was staring at the floor again, hunched over and looking miserable. "Thanks," he barely whispered.

I couldn't stand it and went over to lift his chin. Holding his cheeks in my hands, I stroked him with my thumbs and made him look at me.

"Don't take on the burden of your father's crimes."

"I should've seen—"

"If he didn't want you to know, you never would've."

Owen sighed and relaxed in my hands, his eyes glassy with emotion.

I kissed between his eyes and then rubbed my cheek on the same spot before hugging him close. "That you didn't know should also tell you that he knew you would never consent to what he had planned."

I felt him nod against my chest, and oh how I wished I was naked again so that I could feel him pressed to every inch of my body. Would he enjoy the feel of my fur on his bare skin? Would he pet me as I'd seen Logan pet his prince?

The urge to find out was nearly overwhelming, but I knew I wouldn't be able to stop once I started and there was still so much to do.

I patted Owen and stepped back. Taking some satisfaction that he seemed reluctant to let me go, I said, "I have to go to the bridge and continue monitoring the situation. You can use that same icon to order food, if you wish, and feel free to make use of the facilities."

"But don't leave the room."

"They won't let you without my permission."

"Okay."

His easy acceptance of the parameters of his confinement said more about his lingering guilt than anything else. I reached over and swiped my thumb across his bottom lip before I could stop myself. At the widening of his eyes and his little gasp, I realized what I'd done and turned to flee.

I was in so much trouble.

CHAPTER 4
OWEN

He wanted me. There was comfort in his actions and expressions, but also a burning desire that was easy to recognize even with the captain's nonhuman face. I couldn't deny that I wanted his care and passion, but I didn't deserve it. There was a real possibility that I'd let him do whatever he wanted with me as thanks for not condemning me with my father. The captain could've chosen to shoot me out of an airlock or something, with or without a trial to prove my guilt—I had no idea what Norlon justice was like.

Kinda clear Norlon forgiveness was swift and thorough.

What were my own people thinking?

Too curious to resist and figuring I needed to check-in with someone, I went over to the monitor and tapped the blue icon on the screen. A black and white rabbit appeared and smiled at me.

"Hello, Owen. I'm Kazelle," she said pleasantly. "The captain said you might like to contact someone on Earth. If you give me their telephone number, I can see about making the connection."

I wanted to be excited about the fact that these aliens could adjust their technology to tap into ours, but my insides were twisting at the thought of who I needed to call. I rattled off the number and thanked her.

"That appears to be an iPhone," she said as she tapped at a keyboard, "so I can connect a FaceTime call, if you'd like."

"Can, um, you make it look like the call's from me? I'm not sure he'll answer otherwise." Or at all even if he did see that it was me.

"Yes, of course. I've already cloned your number."

"Okay then. Go ahead." I managed a nod and cleared my throat, bracing myself for Brett Santos, my father's chief of staff, to answer. I regretted the visual as soon as his ruggedly handsome face appeared.

"Jesus Christ, kid, you're alive! There was footage of you dangling from the arms of some fox alien thing like a dead doll. You looked—"

"That was the captain. He's been really good to me," I said defensively.

"Great. Whatever. You need to get back on camera so people know you're not dead." He looked around the room that was bustling with suited people. "Someone find me Givens!"

John Givens was a photographer, so I had to assume Brett wanted me to pose right now.

Before I could protest, Brett asked, "Where's the fox now?"

"Um, on the bridge I think."

"Well, go get him. We need him in the shot to counter the other one."

"I can't leave this room."

"Why the hell not?"

"Because my father is a terrorist who just killed a bunch of people?" I said that a lot louder than I'd meant to, and all of the people in the room behind Brett stopped to stare.

"You listen to me," Brett said in a dangerous tone, "Governor Devin was *not* responsible for his actions. We're still investigating, but there's evidence that he was being manipulated by outside forces and they're the ones who triggered the bomb."

My gumption fizzled under the weight of his conviction in what he was saying. He couldn't even be honest with me and was instead treating me like the opposition. It reminded me of what Py had just said about me never knowing about the plan because my father had known I'd try to stop him.

"Bob and Eric are dead," I told Brett since I wasn't sure if he knew.

He nodded and wiped a hand down his face, looking exhausted now. I almost felt bad for him.

"The news crew up here is asking for permission to keep broadcasting the recovery. I'm guessing they'll want to talk to me at some point."

"Oh, fuck no," he said with sudden venom. "Don't you dare speak to *anyone*. I'm not going to let you tarnish your father's good works. You might've hated him, Owen, but the rest of us didn't and we're not going to let you ruin everything."

I was so shocked, I blurted out, "Ruin everything? He was an ultra-conservative so filled with hatred that he detonated a bomb on an educational mission, Brett. That's literally all he'll ever be remembered for."

He actually snarled at me. "Musted is taking office later today and he will continue our mission," The screen went black as he hung up on me.

To think I'd once had a crush on him. He'd always been charming and cool, in control and respected. Now he was some idiot trying to tell the world a murderer was just misunderstood. And with my father's lieutenant governor taking his place, absolutely nothing would change for the good people of Ohio who weren't consumed by hatred.

I'd accomplished exactly nothing by making that call. Well, I was on Brett's enemies list, but I was pretty sure I'd already been there.

Kazelle suddenly reappeared on the screen. "Would you like to speak to one of our therapists, Owen?"

The sympathy in her eyes nearly broken me, but I shook my head. "Not right now. I think I'll, um, just get cleaned up and stuff."

"Okay. If you need anything else, just tap the blue icon."

I nodded and the screen went black again. I'd never gone through any therapy, having managed to rise above the awful, ultra-conservative things my father had preached throughout my childhood all on my own. I'd gravitated toward artists and scientists all through school and had even gotten degrees in Art History and Biology before going pre-law with the intention to work for somewhere like The Southern Poverty Law Center someday.

While my relationship with my father had been shaky forever because he'd discovered I was nothing like him, I'd honestly thought we'd been making progress recently on him accepting me. He'd talked a good game, but now I had to wonder if he'd been making nice just to lure me to my death.

My god, I was lucky. And I really did need to thank the captain for his part in keeping me alive.

Since he'd said I could use the facilities, I found the bathroom and was glad to see dials and knobs familiar enough that I could get a shower going. It was kind of comforting to do something so normal, and the hot water and spicy-smelling soap chilled me out a little more.

That it was his soap, his scent, turned me on.

I had to remind myself that was allowed—that I didn't need to be ashamed to find an alien attractive. Sure, people like my father thought it was horrific, but after just the little bit of time I'd spent with the captain, I didn't see as many of our differences as I first had back on Earth. He was competent, brave, compassionate, and he was seriously sexy. If the captain liked me, too, well, maybe we could offer each other a distraction.

After my shower, I wrapped a towel around my waist and realized I absolutely did not want to put back on what had once been one of my favorite charcoal twill suits. The wool had that acrid smokey scent lingering on it and wearing it would make me stick out like something foreign if I was ever allowed out with other people. Since I had no idea how I might get my clothes cleaned or maybe borrow something temporary, I went back over to the monitor.

Kazelle smiled at me. "You look like you feel a bit better."

"I do, yeah. Thank you. But I was wondering if I could get my clothes cleaned or borrow some maybe. Is that possible?"

"Yes, of course. There's a small door in the wall of the lavatory where you can place your clothes. They'll be cleaned overnight and returned to the same spot. In the meantime, I'm going to have some items sent up to you. Can you tell me your sizes?"

I gave her my shirt, pant, and shoe sizes and thanked her a lot for all the help. She let me know it wouldn't be long before someone delivered new clothes for me to try on.

"How about a sandwich?" she asked me. "Or some soup?

This is typically when we have our evening meals, so let me send something up for you."

How surreal that I could get a grilled cheese and tomato soup on an alien spaceship. Did they normally eat such things, or had they stocked up just for visiting humans? It was yet another way they were being so kind to us. I sincerely didn't understand how anyone could hate them.

Hours later, a quiet chirping beep woke me, and I looked to the door from my makeshift bed on the couch. My giant fox walked in, the bright light of the hallway illuminating him until the door shut behind him. I could tell he was staring at me, but I needed longer for my eyes to readjust to the low lighting to see more.

When he walked closer, I could hear him taking deep breaths with his nose in the air. Scenting me? I was a little nervous to have him alone with me again because my immediate thought upon seeing him was to get him on top of me. Standing there deep in shadow, he looked still like a soldier, stately but a little dangerous. Desire simmered in my core.

Without really thinking about it, I tossed the blanket aside and watched his golden eyes track over my semi-nude body. But he didn't make a move. What was he waiting for? Was there some kind of something he needed that was alien to me? Or maybe...

I wiggled out of the boxers I hadn't sent to be cleaned so I could have something to wear to bed and dropped them on the floor. Licking my lips, feeling my cock fill under his steady gaze, I made myself relax back. Words wouldn't come because… What was I even supposed to say? I'd never tried to seduce a human, let alone an alien.

With a sudden growl that made me flinch, he lunged forward, his arms penning me in against the couch. "Do you offer yourself freely?" he said through clenched teeth.

I gulped but nodded. "Y-yes."

"Oh goddess, Owen," he practically moaned before he kissed me.

I hadn't really thought he could kiss with a snout like his, but his lips pursed and pressed against mine, teasing them apart. His tongue slipped in and licked around like he was tasting me. The sound out of his throat told me he liked what he tasted.

I made to reach up for him, bring him down on top of me, but the sound of tearing fabric made me pause. His kissing moved to my neck, but though my eyes were open, I still couldn't see much except that his clothes were flying off of him. He was quite possibly tearing his uniform off. A shiver of desire went through me at his urgency and left me gasping.

A moment later he scooped me up from the couch. Arms around his shoulders and legs around his waist, I moaned at the delicious feel of soft, warm fur against my skin. And a long cock stretching up against my belly. I couldn't help making sounds of pleasure as I rubbed myself against him, loving the tickle and the temptation.

He lowered me onto the bed and stood staring down at me. I licked my lips and stared back at him, loving the intensity of his attention and the way he panted. Then suddenly, he stepped over to an alcove beside the bed and snatched up a bottle. Upending it over his palm, he drizzled out a dollop of clear gel. I bit my lip as I watched him smooth it over his upthrust cock and wished I could see better in the semi-darkness of the room.

Py returned to me and was immediately back to kissing me hungrily. I petted the fur at the back of his head and across his shoulders, luxuriating in the sensations, and let him have access to whatever he wanted. He used the lube still on his hand to slick me up, making me moan as I wondered if we'd frot each other to completion.

But then I felt his fingers searching across my asscheek, heading for my hole. I'd never let someone inside me, but I'd used enough toys to know what to do. I hiked my leg up higher at his waist and groaned when he found where to get inside me. Relaxing, I let him in and, god, that was everything I wanted right then—to have that long, slippery dick fill my guts and ruin me for any human lover.

"Yes," I said between panted breaths. "*Please.*"

He was nibbling at my neck with sharp teeth that made me shiver as his finger teased by barely breaching me over and over again. Then I felt him shift his hips and now it was the wet tip of his cock pressing against my hole. It almost felt like he had a little nub on the very end that poked into me like a tiny finger before the bigger, blunter head said hello.

"Oh fuck yes!" I hollered as he eased his cock inside me. When he bit the join of my neck and shoulder like he was holding me still while he worked his hips to push that cock deeper into me, I wailed in such sharp pleasure and clutched him closer to me. "Don't stop," I begged. "Don't *ever* stop."

He didn't. Even when I felt his furry sac against my ass, he kept thrusting with a maddeningly deliberate pace. He was so deep in me it felt like he was in my guts and… Was he getting thicker? How? It felt like he was stretching me wider from the inside even as he kept moving. And that thicker part was practically grinding on my prostate.

"Py. Py!" I hollered as I thrust up to bury him as deep as I could get him, my orgasm suddenly screaming up on me. It took my breath away for a moment, and then I was wailing with the scorching release as he fucked me through it like he really was never going to stop.

Three more powerful thrusts and he lifted his head to groan at the ceiling as he came, his strong body shuddering above me. He looked so wild and beautiful then.

I noticed his arms were trembling as we caught our breaths, him trying to keep his weight off of me. But I wanted it, wanted to feel him everywhere I could, and curled my arms under his to pull him down. Instead of giving in, though, he scooped me in close and turned around to sit on the edge of the bed with me on his lap. His cock was still up my ass and felt… Well, it felt lodged there.

"Forgive me," he said, his voice gravelly, "but I've knotted you."

"Knotted me?"

"A part of my cock swells to keep me bound to my mate."

"Oh," I breathed, realizing I *had* felt him getting bigger inside me, and now that bulge was locking us together.

"It isn't so large that I couldn't— If you wish for me to separate us…"

I smiled against his collarbone. "Stay," I said because it was clear he didn't want to leave my body yet even if he could.

He tightened his arms around me and sighed as he rested his chin on top of my head. I relaxed against him, grateful to finally get the cuddle I'd been missing since he'd left earlier. Whatever happened next, I didn't really care because I'd just lost my virginity and was going to savor the moment with my incredible fox.

CHAPTER 5
PYSINA

Owen trusted me. I could feel it in the way he gave his weight to me, leaning hard despite being curled to keep our bodies aligned. He accepted me as well, allowing me to stay inside him even though my knot wasn't so large that I couldn't separate us. And Goddess, the way he'd reacted as I'd fucked him with my knot…

Gulping back the desire that would only bind us together longer, I turned my mind to a more complicated issue. Namely, the reason for how I'd behaved since waking after the attack with him in my arms. He'd distracted me from my duties all day and been too much to resist when I returned to him. I'd always thought the stories of how quickly my father and grandfather had claimed their mates was a silly joke, just a tall tale they told at gatherings. But now, I couldn't deny that I'd been compelled to make Owen mine.

"I talked to my father's chief of staff earlier," Owen whispered, breaking my train of thought. "It was…bad."

I didn't bother telling him that I knew of everything he'd done since being confined to my quarters or that I could replay the conversation if necessary. Instead, I asked, "What did he say?" I cupped the back of Owen's head protectively.

Disbelief, maybe some disgust, dripped from Owen's voice as he said, "Brett's trying to spin it like my father was a victim. Can you believe that? Like he was somehow coerced into detonating a bomb by some outside force."

"Impossible. We invited him here because of his condemnation of us. We had hoped to enlighten him. He knew what he was doing."

Owen sat back enough to look me in the eye. "Did you suspect he was with Humans First?"

"No." None of the intelligence briefings I had received had ever even hinted at such a connection. "And neither are you."

Owen made an incredulous face. "Of course not," he said as our bodies disconnected on their own. He sighed, and to my ears it sounded disappointed.

Could he feel even a small amount of what I felt for him? The drive to remain by his side? The desperation to mark him as my own? I gently touched where his neck and shoulder met, where I'd bitten him to keep him still as I claimed him.

"Owen," I whispered, forcing myself to say this, "I am very attached to you."

He nodded and reached up to smooth back the short hairs at my cheek. "Yeah. Same."

A shiver I couldn't contain lit through me at his confirmation.

"We don't have to tell anyone," he said, "if you don't want people to know. I'm not exactly a prize at the moment."

That he could say such a thing about himself put a growl in my tone. "You are *not* your father, and I will shred anyone who claims you are. I may not know you well yet, but I already know you are incapable of the sort of hate and destruction that he committed." I took a deep breath as he blinked at me before I drew a fingertip along the evidence of my bite. "Besides, anyone who looks at you will know what this means."

He frowned for a moment before his eyes went wide and he stumbled off my lap. I stayed where I was sitting on the edge of the bed as Owen dashed into the lavatory, probably for a look in the mirror since the light went on. When it turned off again, I braced myself for his admonishment.

Owen walked back to me with his cheeks stained by a blush and a wicked little smile on his lips. He liked my mark. Goddess, but knowing that went straight to my cock.

In a small, shy voice he asked, "Will you do that and the knotting every time?" He stood in front of me looking at me through his long, dark lashes.

"Perhaps not every time." I reached for him, drawing him between my thighs with both hands cupping his ass. "Only when I need to stake my claim."

As sophisticated as we Norlons were, our baser instincts still managed to influence us when it came to our mates. Everything in me demanded I make absolutely certain that everyone knew he was mine. He smelled of me and my lust, but not yet strongly enough. I should take him again.

"So maybe—" He cut himself off with a gasp as I let my claws out to press into his cheeks. Between us, his cock began to stiffen.

"So maybe?" I asked, curious about what he'd been about to say before I'd distracted him. I leaned in and rubbed my cheek against his, transferring more of my scent to his skin.

He pressed his ass back into my hands and shivered as he blinked several times, looking up at the ceiling. He seemed to be trying to take deeper breaths than the panting he was doing. That I could ruin his concentration made me grin.

"So maybe," I teased, "I should claim you again?"

"Oh. Yes, that." He nodded fast and his hands came up to burrow into the hairs at my neck. "That's a *great* idea."

While he petted me—a sensation I hadn't realized I needed so much—I gave in to my instincts and licked him. His neck, the bite, his pair of tiny nipples, the slight ridges of his abdomen… When I could go no lower in that position, I lifted him and turned to deposit him on the bed again. The way he splayed his lean legs open for me and how his cock already leaked with want of my attentions drove me to my knees to continue licking him.

And sucking him. The high-pitched and startled sounds he made as I drew his cock into my mouth was like the most moving piece of music I'd ever heard. I held his thighs spread wide and teased him with the prick of my claws as I squeezed his muscles. His fingers scrabbled at my scalp, tugged my ears, and he wasn't shy about letting me hear his every gasp, holler, and moan.

My Owen was so very responsive, as though I was the first to ever touch him.

When my own desires had me desperate for him, I flipped Owen over onto his stomach and pushed one of his legs up to open him. I growled as I realized I'd put the lubricant back and lunged for it. Sweet Owen didn't move a muscle. Quickly, I slicked myself and, in an instant, I seated myself inside him, my knot already expanding to stretch him open further. Owen wailed his pleasure, humping back against me as I fucked him, my knot no doubt grinding on his most sensitive places in the very best ways.

One of his hands disappeared beneath him, and I assumed

he meant to touch himself to spur on his release. But no, little Owen reached lower to feel where we were joined. His smooth fingertips explored the stretch of his hole and how my cock filled him. I slowed down, savoring his touches, and couldn't resist whispering to him.

"Are you mine, Owen?"

"Oh… Oh god, yeah."

I ground against his fingers, and he moaned wantonly.

"Will you receive me every night?"

He made a whimpering sound and nodded against the bedding. "E-every night. Days, too. When-whenever!"

I could feel he was close to coming and now couldn't resist pinning him again. Biting him had him going stiff beneath me, a wail of release clawing free of his throat as his body shuddered and twitched. My claws sank into the bedding as my own orgasm came upon me and I lifted my head to moan through it, cock buried deep inside him and filling him yet again.

Since I knew he liked the weight of me on him, I stayed where I was as we calmed. He wiggled against me, pressing his ass firmly into my hips as though determined not to lose my cock. He took one of my hands and moved it under his cheek, resting his head on me and closing his eyes with a sigh. My sweet little touch-starved mate… I wrapped more of myself around him, willing to give him whatever he needed for as long as he'd let me.

"Py, this shower isn't big enough for both of us."

Morning had found me waking alone to the sound of

running water, and I'd immediately set out to find the source. With his hair wet and slicked back from his face, Owen's blue eyes were impossibly large as he stared up at me from within the bathing chamber. And when I picked him up and his legs immediately went around my waist as his mouth popped open, his beautiful eyes seemed to grow even bigger.

As did his cock as it pressed against mine.

"Now we fit in here just fine."

He bit his bottom lip as he grinned, fingers smoothing my wet hair back from my face even as his hips rolled to grind us together. I turned and leaned him against the wall of the chamber, making him gasp at the cool material against his skin. Holding onto his ass, I fucked against him, rubbing our wet cocks on our stomachs and watching him gasp and moan.

The water fell across us both, wetting down most of my hair and cascading over his nearly hairless body. Goddess, he was a lovely shade of peach until he slowly deepened to dark pink as his arousal built. He was my first human, and I was desperate to remember all that there was to learn about his desires.

"Py! Ugh… So good." Owen rocked with me, his legs squeezing around me tighter than I'd thought he could. It made my claws come out and prick against the cheeks of his ass. "Yes! Oh fuck, yes!"

Owen coming then threw me over the edge with him, and the scent of our sex filled the small space. I drew in deep breaths of it, savoring how perfect we were together. With a mighty groan, he went limp in my arms except for the occasional muscle twitch, and I held him close as I recognized his trust again.

I had duties to attend to, but oh how I longed to spend the next fortnight bringing off my Owen in every possible way.

"You better have meant it," Owen mumbled, "when you said you were attached because I think I'm addicted."

I smiled against the top of his wet head and maneuvered us under the water before my allotted amount ran out. That Owen claimed such things aloud pleased me greatly and made it easier to set him on his feet so that I might clean him before attending to my day.

"I meant it," I told him as I massaged soap into the wavy locks atop his head. "If I could, I would permanently embed my cock in your ass."

He snorted a laugh before rinsing his hair with a grin on his upturned face. When he added soap to his hands, I expected him to wash the rest of himself, but he looked expectantly up at me. I held my hands out, indicating that he might wash any and every part of me that he wished to touch.

With a giddy little noise, Owen started on my chest by creating a great lather of white bubbles. I stood still as soon as I realized he was also exploring me, letting out a delighted hum when he found each of my six nipples. His hands delved into my hair from shoulders to groin where he fondled my sac and the sheath at the base of my cock. When he reached deeper between my legs, I obliged him by turning around.

Now my tail seemed to fascinate him as he stroked it repeatedly. The suggestive move was not lost on my cock, which rallied eagerly for another round. And when Owen's nimble fingers teased my hole, I briefly reevaluated my preferences.

Owen had me switch places with him to rinse myself as he washed his body like he was in a hurry. His cock was only semi-hard, and I wondered if I had exhausted him. I stepped out of the bathing chamber to allow him to rinse off while I attempted to calm. My baser instincts might be heightened right now, but that didn't mean I had to obey them.

I was standing in front of the dryers when Owen emerged. He wiped water from his eyes and watched me in a way that did not help my erection to abate. Those eyes of his… I would do anything to have them always on me.

"Should I use that, too?" he asked.

It took me a moment to understand what he meant. "The dryers? Yes, of course." I moved out of the way so that he could stand in front of them now.

He needed far less time in the path of the warm air to dry his bare skin, and his hair was a wild mass of silky black waves once he was done. He laughed at himself as he peered into the mirror, but then his fingers traced over the twin sets of bite marks on his shoulders. He bit his bottom lip and grinned at me in the reflection.

Then he was suddenly on his knees in front of me.

CHAPTER 6
OWEN

Seeing the marks Py had left on my skin got me hot all over again. And since his cock hadn't retreated into the furry cream-colored sheath at his groin, I couldn't resist dropping to my knees in front of him. Py stared down at me with wide eyes and his cock perked right up to point toward me, making me smile. As soon as I leaned in and lapped at the cute little protrusion from the head of his cock, he palmed the back of my head.

I shivered when I felt the tiniest prick of his claws on my scalp. Why the threat of them thrilled me so much, I had no idea. I'd never fantasized about pain with sex, but the little bit of scratch and those bites really revved me up. But I ignored my own growing interest and took advantage of the chance to explore him some more.

Three pairs of nipples? Awesome. All this fur? Fantastic! And now I had a tube-like protrusion from the fat head of his cock to tease with my tongue, a firm shaft covered in pulsing veins, and that wicked knot already plumping up as I investigated every inch of him. His wasn't a human cock, and I loved it.

When I took his dick into my mouth, my lips bumped against the knot, and Py sucked in a breath as his claws squeezed my head. I wasn't going to attempt to fit the knot in my mouth, but I moaned as I remembered vividly how he'd been able to keep fucking me even as it had swelled inside me. The way it had teased my prostate? Fuck... I pulled off to angle his dick to the side so that I could lave at the knot with all the gratitude I could express with lips and tongue.

Py was still staring down at me, so I kept as much eye contact as I could with him. He was panting, that extra bit on the tip of his dick already leaking. He tasted sort of salty-sweet, and I liked it.

My wandering hands found his furry sac tucked up high between his slightly trembling legs, and wow was the fur there super soft. I bobbed on his dick, fondled him, and couldn't resist reaching down to stroke myself.

"Owen," he growled, "don't come."

Don't come? I looked up at him and stopped jerking myself.

"Save it for me," he said and flexed his claws through my hair.

I shivered and closed my eyes as the possibilities of how he'd take care of me after he came swirled through my mind. Locking eyes with him again, I redoubled my efforts to suck him off and gripped the firm globes of his furry ass.

This wasn't my first time blowing someone, but it was the first time it might just get me off, too. Watching him stare at me, hearing him whine and moan because of what I was doing to him, and feeling him tremble and twitch was incredible in ways I hadn't known before. Everything I was doing was driving him crazy with lust—I could see it in his eyes and the way his lip would curl now and then in a snarl of need.

Py *desired* me.

"Owen!" he hollered before his claws scratched and he pulled me onto his dick. Lips pressed to his knot and his cock nearly in my throat, I held my breath and tried to open up more for him. Warm spurts hit the back of my tongue and slithered down my throat. I shivered as I stared up at him, memorizing the way he seemed so desperate to keep watching me. It made me feel powerful and necessary.

With a gasp, he held onto my shoulder and eased me back. I sucked in a breath, too, and licked my lips as I gazed adoringly at his deep red cock. Was it weird to consider it mine now? Like I'd claimed it? Because if anyone else ever attempted to do this with him, I'd scratch their eyes out.

Suddenly, Py bent and scooped me up to set my naked ass on the counter. I gasped from the chill, and then hollered when he leaned over me and sucked my whole cock into his mouth. With his snout, I probably wasn't anywhere near his throat, but his lips tightened perfectly and his tongue swirled all around me. Even the threat of his pointy teeth was doing it for me.

Then he went and pressed a hand to my chest, making me lean against the mirror behind me. It was as if he felt the need to hold me down.

I came so fast, I didn't even have a chance to warn him.

"Oh fuck. Oh my god," I said through full-body twitches as he sucked every last drop out of me.

Py pulled off slowly, which made me holler from sensation overload. He knew it, too, because he was smirking when he looked me in the eyes. I huffed a weak laugh and caught his furry cheeks in my hands to draw him closer for a kiss. Honestly, I could spend hours just petting him—he was so soft. I looked forward to curling up with him again tonight.

In the meantime, I had to get through another day. When Py turned to dress, he found that clothes had been delivered for me. Though they were a bit big on me, wearing them made me look like I belonged. Made me feel like I did, too. Everyone not in uniform wore a tunic over skintight pants with little slip-on shoes that reminded me of ballet flats. My outfit was a pale lime green, like a peridot, that looked really good on me. I wouldn't stand out as one of the visiting humans if I walked around the ship.

"Can I leave the room today?" I asked Py as I admired the beadwork on my tunic. For something on loan to me, it was pretty fancy.

"You can. Why not start by going to the commissary for breakfast?"

"Okay, I can do that."

At the door, Py gave me another kiss that the uniformed rabbit waiting in the hall definitely didn't miss. They didn't say a word—probably out of respect for their boss—and Py told them to escort me to the commissary. I stood there watching him walk away, the swish of his orange and white tail mesmerizing me as much as the bunch and flex of his ass in tight black pants. When he rounded a corner out of sight, I remembered my escort and felt a blush heat my face.

"This way, sir." They gestured in the opposite direction.

"I'm Owen Devin." I said as we walked along. "What's your name?"

"Ensign Laray Codisin. I'm a Pip."

They had dark brown fur and one long ear that stood up while the other folded over halfway down. It made them look like they were forever curious. My fingers itched to find out if they were softer than Py, but petting them seemed really rude, like something way too intimate for a brand-new acquaintance. I resisted.

But since I had someone who was kind of impartial, I made myself speak up. "Can I ask... Um..." I cleared my throat. "Are Norlons okay with someone having a relationship with a human?"

"As okay with it as we would be if he was involved with someone who wasn't a Lago like himself." They shrugged one shoulder and gestured for us to get into the lift. "It presents the same challenges for having offspring and there are cultural differences to contend with, but no one will be upset by the match."

"Challenges? Like what?"

"Oh, none of us are genetically compatible with the others. If I were to mate with a Yook, for example, we'd have to consider other ways to bring children into our lives. The same goes for humans."

"Huh, I hadn't considered that." And was oddly disappointed that wolf-bunny hybrids couldn't be a thing. "Still, though, it's reassuring that mixed relationships aren't a problem in Norlon culture. Thanks."

Ensign Codisin bumped my shoulder and grinned when I looked up. "That's not to say a few people won't be jealous and disappointed that he's taken, though. The captain's been notoriously difficult to bed."

I blushed and couldn't help chuckling since Py had been crazy easy to seduce last night. As delightful as it was to have caught the uncatchable, it was also sobering to think that our instant connection was that powerful. Like was it a pheromone that had us into each other so fast? Or was it more magical, like fate?

My thoughts were interrupted when I stepped into the commissary and realized all the other visiting humans were there as well. It must've been late for breakfast by ship standards, too, because we were literally the only people present. There was no crowd for me to get lost in so that I could avoid everyone.

Ensign Codisin led me over to the cafeteria-style buffet where a tiger-type Khess smiled at me. "Welcome! We have a selection of American breakfast foods available for you, but if you'd like to try Norlon dishes, I can help you understand them."

"Oh, um, this is perfect. Thank you." I went down the line with them, selecting scrambled eggs with cheddar cheese, a waffle with maple syrup, and several slices of thick-cut bacon. At the end, I got a glass of water and another of orange juice before I was forced to turn around and find a table.

I was suddenly flung back in time to every new year at boarding school and that first meal where everyone was eyeing up everyone else. Only this time, it was entirely possibly every single person hated me. Gulping as I saw that several people watched me, I tried not to run as I went for an empty table.

Ensign Codisin didn't join me, instead going over to stand with other uniformed Norlons who might've escorted the rest of the visitors here. They sipped steaming mugs and chatted like absolutely nothing was wrong. I wondered if my ensign would intervene if someone rushed me.

I'd managed two bites of egg when three people got up and came over. What if they were angry about what my father had done? Would they blame me? Test my loyalty to him? I sat there frozen and staring as all three of them sat down at the table.

"You're Owen Devin, right?" a dark-haired man asked. I

didn't know exactly who he was, but he'd been talking into the camera on the trip up here, so I assumed he was an anchor for PBS News.

I nodded at him.

"Last time I saw you," he went on, "it looked like you were unconscious or dead. It's good to see that you're okay."

It was? I glanced at the other two, an Asian woman and another dark-haired man. I was no expert on facial expressions, but it kind of looked like all of them were concerned. Which didn't make sense. Why weren't they mad?

"The two men who passed," the woman said, "I assume you knew them?"

"Bob and Eric?" I said, surprised.

"Right. You have our sympathies for their losses, too."

Holy shit. They were offering their condolences to me. No malice or anger at all.

"Um, thank you. I, uh, I'm sorry about my father." That felt like such a lame thing to say, but what else could I do? "I'm sorry I didn't know he was that dangerous."

The first man sighed heavily. "It's tough, feeling responsible for someone like that, but we knew your relationship with him had been strained for a lot of years."

Right, I'd almost forgotten that these were reporters. They might've known more about my father than I had.

"Oh," the man said and stuck out his hand. "I'm Doug Fowkes, anchor for PBS News up here."

"Owen," I said automatically as I shook his hand.

The woman was Ashley Wong, a producer, and the other man was Todd Barnes, a cameraman.

"Any chance you'd do a segment with us?" Ashley asked. "We're interviewing everyone who's able and sharing the footage with the surface. Nothing's live," she hastened to add.

I gulped and grabbed my juice since it suddenly felt like some egg was lodged in my throat. Could I do an interview? Fuck, I wasn't sure I could. Even if it was just me in a recorded segment, the story would be picked up by every other station and dissected by their talking heads and so-called experts. The right-wing media would eviscerate me.

"Can I think about it?" I managed to ask.

Ashley patted my arm. "Of course! Take your time. But you are the one that everyone's desperate to hear from, Owen. We want to know what you know."

It might've been easier if they'd just gotten mad at me.

CHAPTER 7
PYSINA

Two days later, after Owen left our quarters to get breakfast with his escort, I placed a call to my family home back on Nor. I'd let them know I was fine after the bomb so they wouldn't worry, but now I had questions for my father about being mated. Worries and fears that I hoped he could abate.

"Pysina!" he said with a beaming smile the second the connection established. He smoothed back the white hairs around his mouth, and I knew he'd probably just had a torsa cake, his favorite snack. "How are you? No more explosions, I trust?"

I resisted rolling my eyes. "No more explosions, Father."

He squinted at the screen. "Then tell me why your frown lines seem deeper than usual. Are the humans misbehaving? Are you making less progress?"

I ignored his questions since he knew I wasn't actively involved with the delegation and got straight to the point instead. "I've found my mate in one of the visiting humans. A man named Owen Devin."

His eyes slowly widened and his mouth popped open before he suddenly hollered, "Feesia! Connect in! He's found his mate!"

I sighed. I should've known he'd make a thing of it. While the background behind him seemed to indicate that he was out in the back garden, my mother joined from her workshop, paint already streaking her face.

"A mate?" she said in lieu of greeting. "Who is it? You haven't told us about anyone since that Khess who broke—"

"They're a human man," Father interrupted. "Straight up from the surface! What was his name again? Oden?"

"Owen," I said patiently.

Mother made a whining sound and clasped both hands against her chest. "Finding love during such trying times... How romantic!"

I shifted around and cleared my throat. "Actually, that's one of the reasons I wanted to discuss this with…you." I'd wanted my father's perspective since he'd been the one to recognize that they were mates long before Mother accepted it, but I couldn't cut her out of the conversation now.

"Mmm, yes," Father said, "that does add another layer of complexity."

At least he understood. "On top of this being my first mating, him being human and only knowing Norlons exist for the past few months, and his father having been the bomber…"

"Oh dear," Mother whispered.

"Well, let's focus on one thing at a time," Father said, and I was relieved to hear it. "As a first mating, you're probably questioning everything you're doing—but don't. Fate has seen fit to toss the two of you together, so trust that your compatibility is infinite. Your instincts will guide you, and you need to listen to them."

While Mother nodded in clear agreement, I considered what my instincts had been telling me so far. In truth, it wasn't much beyond marking and claiming Owen as often as possible. Well, no, over the past two days we'd discussed his concerns over how the other visiting humans perceived him, whether he should talk to the news crew officially, and what he was learning about Norlon culture and our offerings to the humans of Earth. I'd been honest with him during every conversation, so I must've been trusting my instincts there as well as in bed.

"And don't worry about him being human," Father continued. "They aren't so different from us. I think you might need to watch your claws and teeth a bit more than normal, but if your instincts say to do something, do it."

"Exactly," Mother said. "My friend Ipsy—you know Ipsy—her mate is human and she said he never responds better than when she treats him no differently than any other Norlon lover she's ever had."

I didn't want to discuss with my parents the details of my sex life with my new mate—or Ipsy's with hers—but what they were saying made sense. Every encounter I'd had with Owen had seen me following my urges, and Owen had reacted with hearty approval each time. I wasn't holding back my claws and teeth because he loved to feel them on his delicate skin, so I didn't need to worry about that either.

"Trust in our compatibility," I said with a nod.

"Too right," Father said. "Communication is key, of course, and much of that isn't spoken, but you're together for a reason. This business with his father, though…"

"Owen holds not a single one of his father's beliefs," I said, feeling suddenly defensive of him.

"Of course not," they said at the same time.

"Fate," Father said, "wouldn't pit you against an adversary as mate. Trust your instincts while you help him grieve, as well. You're excellent with emotional support."

"He really is," Mother cooed.

Father wiggled closer to the screen, grinning. "Now tell me all about your Owen."

Heartened that I wasn't doing anything wrong, I spent the next several minutes describing Owen to the delight of both my parents. We all agreed that his gentleness and need for compassion and support was the perfect fit for my rougher nature and desire to uplift those around me.

I didn't tell them about his submissiveness in bed and how his sweet, slim body seemed made to receive me, but I was sure they could guess that we were an exact match there as well.

OWEN

I saw Doug and Ashley in the commissary again, but this time, they didn't come over to sit with me. It had become a regular thing, several of us gathering whenever we found ourselves in there at the same time. We'd chat about innocent things, nothing about the bomb or politics. That they'd broken with tradition made me wonder if they'd given up on getting an interview out of me.

I was a little disappointed that friendship hadn't been what we'd been doing, but also... Maybe it was time to stop avoiding the issue. Maybe I just needed to rip the bandage off and really talk to them.

I couldn't eat anything after that, a turn of events that Ensign Codisin mentioned as we were the last to leave the commissary. "Are you alright, Owen? You hardly ate."

I had to clear my throat a couple of times before I could say, "Can you take me to wherever the news crew is filming?"

They patted my back and changed direction.

By the time we arrived outside a set of double doors with a human standing in front of them, my heart was pounding and my hands were sweating. Could you die from trembling? Maybe I'd pass out first and go peacefully.

"Hi there," a woman my age said with a smile as she flung long braids over her shoulder. "I'm Sandra, an intern with PBS News. How can I help you?"

I kind of croaked at her before clearing my throat. "I'd like to talk to—"

She held up a finger. "We're filming a segment inside, so please keep your voice low."

"Oh, sorry." That explained her own low tone. "Um, I wanted to talk to Doug or Ashley."

"About your experience the other day?"

She didn't recognize me. Normally, I'd be thrilled by that, but it probably wasn't something that would last much longer.

"I'm Owen Devin."

The only thing that betrayed her surprise was a brief hop of her eyebrows. Her smile remained fixed, and I had a feeling she'd be a great news anchor someday.

"Okay," she said. "Hold on one second."

She slipped through the doors, leaving me alone with the ensign.

"You don't have to stay," I said quietly up at Ensign Codisin. "I'll go inside in a minute here. Probably. Unless they don't want me to anymore? I don't know actually. But I'd just go back to the room in that case. You've probably got better—"

"It's okay, Owen. I'll stay," they said with a small smile.

I sighed. "Thanks."

Suddenly, Sandra opened one door wide and waved to us. "Come on in."

I stepped inside but stopped short when I saw Brett's giant head on the screen attached to the opposite wall. He hadn't seen me yet because he was talking to someone near him about a quote on a piece of paper he held up. Had Doug and Ashley given up on me and turned to him instead?

"Owen, hey." Doug came over with a smile on his face and his hand out to shake. "Thanks so much for coming in."

I nodded and managed to shake his hand, but all I could think about was what would happen when Brett saw me. I hadn't thought I'd have to confront him live like this. Was I up for such a fight?

"Listen," Doug practically whispered. "I saw you throw yourself on the captain when the bomb went off, so I understand your stance on Norlon relations. We'd really like to show the public that you're on their side."

That's what he thought I had done? I knew I'd run for Py, but had protecting *him* been any part of my motivation? Because I'd been pretty sure I wanted someone to protect *me*. And now I really didn't want to admit that.

"But Santos here is, uh, spinning things a bit—"

"Oh, I know," I said a little breathlessly before clearing my throat. "I spoke to him the day it happened. He's, um, not going to like me being here."

Doug nodded, studying me. He didn't look any more sure that I could handle this than I felt myself. But dammit I had to speak up. I couldn't let Brett or anyone else on my father's team lie about what he'd done. I *had* to do this.

"Screw it," I said. "I'm here to tell the truth."

CHAPTER 8
OWEN

Predictably, Brett got mad the second he noticed me, and then he demanded to talk to Doug without me being able to hear them. I felt bad letting Doug handle it, but the rest of me was hoping Brett might storm off and that would be the end of it. I'd seen opposition interviews where they brought on people representing two sides of a serious issue. I had a feeling that was what they wanted to do with me and Brett.

Soon enough, I discovered I was right.

While someone toned down the shine of my skin and another person put a mic on me, Ashley quietly explained her vision.

"We have about ten minutes of Doug and Santos, but I'm willing to scrap it all to have you tell your side and get his reactions." She looked over her shoulder at the empty space where Brett had been before staring at me again. "I have a feeling this could get volatile, but it's not live and we'll cut it if he goes too far."

I gulped, having not realized live might've been an option and now wondering what "too far" might mean. I was sure

Brett was against Norlons, but could he blow something up, too? At least he was down there where they weren't.

Ashley was studying me again, so I nodded. "I'll be fine."

She looked relieved as she smiled and gave me a double thumbs-up before moving behind the cameras. Directed to a chair by yet another crew member, I noticed that Ensign Codisin was still in the room and the only Norlon present. Were they more than my escort? Were they maybe a bodyguard, too? Even though Brett wasn't even on the ship, I felt a little better knowing Ensign Codisin might whisk me from the room if things got dangerous.

That fantasy would be even better if it was Py doing the whisking, of course.

"Okay, Owen," Doug said, "we're ready for you."

On the screen, Brett's expression went from frowning menace to sparkling smile. There was the smooth operator who'd once coerced a younger me into giving him a blowjob so that he could confirm my sexuality to my father and remove me as part of the campaign. Strangely, seeing Brett in professional douche mode had a calming effect on me and I sat down in the indicated seat with a smile of my own.

Doug did introductory things like he was kicking off a show before turning his attention to me. "While we have the scene on film, I'd like to get your take on what happened that day. Can you tell me what you experienced, Owen?"

"Well," Brett interrupted, "like all of us, Owen was justifiably startled by—"

"I'm sorry," Doug jumped in, "but I'd like to hear from Owen."

I waited a few heartbeats for Brett to push back, but he simply smiled again, like a viper waiting to strike. My building hatred for him made me brave.

"At first," I said, "I was caught up in how amazing it was to be on a spaceship. I'm still struck by moments of disbelief that this is all real."

Doug chuckled. "Same. It trips you up now and then."

"It does, yeah. So when I walked down the shuttle's ramp, I was staring all around me, taking everything in as fast as I could." I gulped as the memories hit hard. "And then my father said—"

"Allegedly said," Brett snapped.

I frowned at him. "That he said 'Humans First' is a fact, not a rumor. The whole thing was recorded." And I may not have watched it, but I was sure it had been playing on every news station the world over on a damn loop.

Brett shook his head. "Those recordings could've been doctored by any number of bad actors."

"What? I was there! I heard him say Humans First—"

"No, that's not—"

"—before he detonated a bomb! People have *died*, and it's because of my father's actions," I said over Brett's continuing attempts to deny everything. "Two members of his team died in the blast, and I have no doubt he was hoping he'd kill me, too!"

In the silence that followed, I sat there shaking and flushed, sweating suddenly in the wake of speaking that thought out loud. We might not be live, but I knew that would be the soundbite everyone would replay.

Brett lost it. "Only because you're a little queer whore," he snarled. "You've already let one of those animals chew on you, haven't you? I can see the marks. You're nothing but a *freak*, like that other one." He stood up out of frame and shouted, "Cut the feed!"

Py's bite marks. I closed my eyes and sighed as I slumped

in my seat. I hadn't given a single thought to the fact that they might be visible given the low cut of my tunic's collar. And I'd been proud of them until now.

Sure, it was possible Doug and the crew wouldn't air that outburst, but everyone in the room now knew I was gay and had done something with one of the Norlons. Ensign Codisin probably had no doubt who, and I worried that I might tarnish Py's reputation. Maybe even obliterate it. We might be great together, but that didn't mean we should keep seeing each other.

"Owen," Doug said quietly.

I swallowed hard and looked at him. "I'm sorry. I can explain."

But he shook his head. "We're not in the business of involuntarily outing people, so we won't air that. You have nothing to apologize for or explain."

I could've cried in gratitude and rubbed at my eyes hard to try and disguise that. I'd probably never given PBS News a single thought, but goddamn, they were my favorites now. "Thank you," I whispered.

"Let's start again," Ashley said with a nod toward Doug. "Santos can go on Fox News to peddle his bullshit."

Doug's smile was calculated as he turned to look at me. "How about it, Owen? Want to start over, just the two of us?"

While the second version of my interview proved to be way better than the first one, we still talked about the possibility that my father might've brought me along so he could kill me with the rest of his enemies. I'd cried talking to Doug about everything and even come out in order to explain why my father had hated me. Brett and those who'd loved my father's politics would pick up the torch and come after me, no doubt, but maybe I just wouldn't ever go back.

What was even down there for me anyway? Like my father's legacy would be his final act, mine would forever be tied to him. I was the one who hadn't known, hadn't died. I could go back home and get my law degree, pass the bar, and join a liberal firm working to beat back people like Brett. But it would always come up that I was my father's son.

Up here, with Py, I could reinvent myself and get away from all of that.

Something else Doug and I had talked about were a few of the programs the Norlons were still successfully running on Earth, including the recruitment of human sex workers. Clearly, I didn't mind sex with a Norlon, so maybe I could…

But no. It wasn't just anyone that had my attention and interest. As I left the interview, the only Norlon I wanted to be near was Py. And not even to fuck him! I really wanted one of his incredibly soft and warm hugs.

"Could you take me to P— Captain Langarus?" I asked Ensign Codisin as my cheeks heated.

They stared at me for a moment, whiskered bunny nose twitching. They had, of course, heard everything from the interview, so I knew they could guess why I wanted Py. "He's probably on the bridge and may not be available, but we can try."

I nodded since that made total sense. "Thanks."

The journey took us down corridors and onto lifts, and I was lost within seconds. Like I seriously could not have gotten myself back to the conference room Doug and the others were using, let alone Py's quarters. It made me smile to think that I was under lock and key but had no idea how to go anywhere.

What I saw on the way was a lot of interior grayish walls with warm lighting and darker tile floors. It definitely felt like we were heading into the more functional areas of the ship, and there were a lot more people in uniform here, too.

I started feeling like I was one hundred percent going to interrupt something far more important than my fragile emotional state. I should turn around and go back to the room. Just when I was about to tell Ensign Codisin to forget about it, we stopped outside a door that didn't automatically open for us. A voice said something in a language I didn't understand, and the ensign had a brief conversation with whoever that was.

"They're checking," Ensign Codisin said.

"Oh. Okay."

How weird that it hadn't occurred to me until now that the Norlons had their own language. Of course they did. Any of them that had spoken English around me had probably done so to include me in the conversation. Which was an example of how inclusive they wanted to be. Norlons might have their faults, but they were just *so nice*.

Suddenly, the door gave a hiss and separated, each side sliding away to reveal a lot of people doing various tasks while either looking at their own smaller screens or the big one on the wall in front of them. It was clean and bright, definitely sci-fi in its level of tech, with everyone speaking that other language in calm, low tones. I hesitated to walk in.

"Owen."

My attention snapped to the other side of the room where Py stood in a doorway. His expression was curious, so at least he wasn't annoyed that I was visiting him at work. Like a dork, though, I just waved at him before I realized I should probably go to him.

He gave me a little smile before stepping back into the other room so I could follow him inside. Only then did I realize this had to be his office. Warm colors, a few knick-knacks, three things that looked like they might be awards, and even a few strange plants decorated the space. It felt a lot like his quarters.

"Are you alright?" he asked as the door shut.

I felt like an idiot as I said, "I just…wanted to see you. After the interview and stuff."

He sat on the edge of his desk, making us eye level. "You did the interview?"

"Yeah. It was time."

"Did something upset you?"

I shrugged. "Parts of it, yeah. I mean most of it, I guess."

"Were they respectful?"

"Oh, yeah. Doug was great, actually. They were interviewing Brett when I arrived. My father's chief of staff?" I said since I couldn't remember if I'd told Py his name before or not. Py nodded. "Anyway, he said some wrong and hurtful things, and they're basically not going to air anything he said now. They knew he was lying, too."

"That's good."

"It is."

I wasn't sure what to do with my hands and ended up crossing my arms as I stared at the floor between his feet. He had huge, paw-like feet despite his hands looking like mine, and his boots reflected that fact. They were very shiny and black and, though I couldn't see myself while standing, I bet I could if I got closer.

"Did you want to talk about what was said?" Py asked.

I wasn't sure, but I knew he was trying to be helpful, even though I wasn't giving him much to work with. I shrugged at him.

Py stood up and started unbuttoning the red jacket of his uniform. Obviously, I wouldn't mind a show, but… "What are you doing?"

He spread the sides of the jacket open. "Come to me."

Not one to turn away getting close to his furriness, I walked over and into his arms, getting that hug I'd wanted. Immediately, he adjusted my position so that my face was pressed between his soft, furry pecs. I didn't resist since it was a nice place to be and… Okay, it was chilling me out a lot because he wrapped one arm around me and held the back of my head with his other hand. Breathing in the spicy, warm scent of him, I felt comforted and protected.

And Py had known that I needed that.

"Hank ooo," I tried to say.

He relaxed his grip on me. "What?"

I turned my head to the side but stayed plastered to him. "Thank you."

CHAPTER 9
PYSINA

Sweet little Owen. I rested my chin on his head and kept my hold on him firm so that he would know he was safe. My instinct to give him direct access to my scent and heat seemed to be helping him as well.

I was going to have to tell my parents that they'd been right.

"Of course," I said after Owen thanked me. It seemed as though comfort or reassurance was not something he was used to having.

Owen sighed heavily. "I think my father invited me up here with him so he could kill me, too."

It felt as though everything in me paused in horror. His father had wanted him dead? My Owen? How could a parent ever feel that way about their child?

"Goddess, why?" I couldn't stop my claws from extending as I gripped Owen a little tighter.

He turned to press his forehead against my chest. "We were never the same after he found out I was gay. I was tricked into revealing that because I knew he wouldn't be happy and couldn't accept me. I just didn't realize…" He sighed again and leaned more against me. "I never suspected he'd want me dead."

I held his face in my hands and made him look up at me. "You are perfect just as you are, Owen. He was wrong about you in every way. Do you hear me?"

He smiled and there was a soft expression in his eyes. "I hear you."

I clutched him to me again, claws pricking into his clothes as I held him. The position of us reminded me of how I'd stood holding him in the landing bay. Right after his father had tried to kill him. Thank the goddess that fucking human hadn't succeeded.

Owen adjusted his stance, and I felt his cock firming against my thigh. Which part of this was arousing him, I didn't know, but I reached down to palm his ass and grind him on me. A breathy moan left him as his arms went from tucked along my abs to sliding behind me. His little fingers sifted my hair between them, petting me and moaning again.

I shouldn't even consider taking him in my office. The wall into the rest of the bridge wasn't thick enough to stop anyone from hearing us—it was designed for exclamations to reach me before an alarm could sound. Owen was not quiet. My crew would know.

And, goddess, I didn't care.

Rucking up Owen's tunic, I shoved a hand down the back of his very tight pants to fit a finger between his cheeks. He gasped, his hips bucking forward before he pushed back and rode my finger. Careful of my claw, I delved deeper until I could press the pad of my finger to his hole.

"Oh, fuck," he groaned. "Please, Py. Please!"

I slipped away from him, circling around, and planted his hands on the top of my desk. I watched him bite his bottom lip as a full-body shiver overtook him. His easy submission went straight to my cock.

"Undress," I told him. Unable to retract my claws in such a state, I could only concentrate on not ruining my uniform—he'd have to see to his own clothes if he wanted them to stay in one piece.

And as if I'd known this day might come, I opened a small panel in my desk and drew out the single-use tube of lubricant that I'd stashed there once upon a time.

Owen tore his tunic up and over his head, flinging it to the floor before wrestling his waistband down. When it cleared his ass, those luscious globes bouncing for a moment, I licked my lips and decided on what I would do to him first. He actually growled in frustration getting his pants to his ankles before he ripped them off, his shoes flying. Such a show of eagerness was a testament to how much he wanted me.

Hands planted again on the surface of my desk, Owen leaned over and widened his legs. He looked back at me, expression curious and gaze flicking down to my freed cock already hard and glistening for him.

I went to my knees behind him.

Owen's surprised gasp made me grin as I used my thumbs to spread his cheeks and reveal his hole. Leaning in close, I licked him from balls to back and reveled in the needy whine out of him. I closed my eyes and concentrated on the feel of his pulsing pucker on my tongue and the scent of his building desire. Owen was not quiet or still and both grew in volume and activity when I gripped his hips, my claws making a series of small indentations in his perfect flanks.

There was no way my crew could misinterpret what was happening in here. Part of me felt proud to pleasure a mate so well that he was unable to control himself. Hopefully, my crew would be secretly and silently impressed.

When I had Owen's hole looser and wet, my tongue corkscrewing in and out of him with ease, he stopped moaning and started begging.

"Py! Oh god, *please*. Please! I'm gonna come."

That last phrase felt like a threat, so I stood and opened the tube to slather its contents on my straining cock. "You'll come with me or not at all."

He made a loud, frustrated noise. "Then fuck me, dammit!"

Pleased by his desperation, I pushed into him slowly and leaned over his back. He shivered hard and tipped up to receive me.

"I won't fuck you," I whispered in his ear. "But I will claim you. You're mine, Owen Devin. All mine."

I wasn't prepared for him to make a sad little sound as I seated myself inside him fully. He squeezed his eyes closed and bit his lip, turning his face into the desk, and trying to hide behind his arms. I stilled, watching, and tried to understand what had moved him to such despair.

Quietly, I asked him, "Do you want me to stop?"

"No." He shook his head almost violently. "Please, don't stop claiming me."

Claiming him. It hit me then that he'd spent the morning being rejected by people he knew and confronting the terrible realization that his father might've wished him dead. Yet here I was accepting him and making him mine.

I rested more fully on top of him, sharing heat and weight, as I penned him in beneath me. "Sweet Owen, no one else can have you, and no one else will have me but you." I moved inside him, gratified by his soft moan. "Never forget that we belong together and I am forever your champion."

He sniffed and found my hand, bringing the back of it to his lips. He swallowed a few times and seemed to struggle to find words, but I didn't need him to speak. He turned his little hand over beneath mine and laced our fingers together, palm to palm, and that said everything to me.

Knowing he liked it, I set my teeth to his neck and held him down as I gave myself over to thrusting into him. Owen gasped and whined, bucking up to draw me deeper, and rocking with me. When he reached up to grab my ear and hold me where I was, I chuckled around my mouthful of his flesh and rode him harder.

He came with a yell, his body squeezing so tightly around me. I shoved into him as deep as I could and lifted my head to holler with my own release. Two short barks slipped out, and I tucked my face against the back of neck in sudden embarrassment. Owen said nothing, probably because he didn't know how primitive that was of me. He sighed in obvious bliss, a smile curling the corner of his mouth, so perhaps I shouldn't be ashamed of such a reaction.

"I really love that knot," he said with his eyes still closed.

"This one?" I teased as I thrust just a bit.

He gasped before moaning wantonly. "Y-yeah, that's it."

Other partners had complained that my knot wasn't big enough to immobilize me within them, but Owen loved that it didn't. I rocked against him a few more times. It was clear to me now that my knot brutally teased his prostate as he twitched and cried out beneath me. When he slammed a fist against the desktop, I stopped and began gently withdrawing. He gave a little whine, but I knew he'd had enough.

As I stood over his limp, flushed form, I smiled with the pride brimming inside me for having claimed my mate so thoroughly.

Unfortunately, a low alert drew my attention to the other side of my desk. Owen looked up, and I touched a finger to my lips as I pressed the icon to speak. "Yes?"

"Sir," Lieutenant Commander Rigger said, "the prince would like to speak with you when you have a moment."

"Let him know I'll meet him in his quarters shortly." Because I couldn't have him in here until the air filters had done away with the scent of sex.

"Yes, sir."

Owen's eyes were huge as he slowly stood up. "We shouldn't have done this in here, huh?"

I waved that away as I walked toward the ensuite. "I don't regret a moment of time spent with you."

I cleaned myself up and straightened my clothes before he appeared in the doorway with an adorable grin on his bite-swollen lips. I leaned down and kissed him, promising myself that the next time his lips were red and puffy would be because I'd kissed them so much and not because he'd worried them that way.

"Get cleaned up," I told him, "and then I'll have your escort take you to visit Logan."

We traded places so I could wipe the front of my desk clean of his release. I didn't truly disinfect the spot because I didn't have such supplies, and a feral part of me enjoyed knowing he'd marked this room.

"Who's Logan?" Owen asked as he came back out and went to retrieve his pants.

"Another Earth human and the prince's mate. He has been instrumental in assisting us with our efforts to integrate with your planet." I tossed the cleaning cloth in the trash and studied Owen. "I thought perhaps you could speak to him about joining the delegation since you understand human politics."

Owen paused in pulling up his pants to blink at me. "Oh."

"If you would rather not, then—"

"No, I will." He returned to dressing, a thoughtful expression on his face. "I hadn't really thought about being useful, but I'd like to be."

"Good." We needed all the help we could get, and maybe working with Logan would give Owen a purpose that might show him his own worth.

CHAPTER 10
OWEN

My face was in flames as Py and I left his office. Even though no one looked at us with a raised eyebrow or even a hint of a smirk, I couldn't help but feel like they knew exactly what had happened in there. Well, okay, maybe not all of it.

I'd never cried during sex before. Py had responded to my tears just perfectly, and I knew he'd meant it when he'd said I was his. And that he was my champion? God, I could cry all over again just about that. Part of me felt so pathetic that I'd never had someone say such a thing to me. No one had ever been that deep in my corner with me.

I was going to fall for him. Actually, I was already falling.

Gulping at that realization, I put a hand over my heart. I'd never been in love before. Was this really how it felt? I wanted to be with Py, help him succeed, and be his champion right back. Did that equal love? I didn't know how I was supposed to be sure, but I could practically feel the hearts in my eyes as I gazed at his back.

Ensign Codisin walked beside me as we followed Py and a small collection of people who kept popping out and needing a word with him. It was amazing to watch him work—he always sorted out whatever business they brought him and even sent them to a better person than him to help them. And the fact that he'd speak English the entire time made me think he was trying to include me. More heart eyes.

Though the ensign would be leaving me since their watch was over, we were all going to the prince's quarters because Logan was there waiting with the prince. Putting aside my squishy heart, I tried to focus on meeting royalty and making myself useful.

So much could be riding on how this meeting went. Maybe it was the prince who wanted me tagged and escorted. Meeting me might mean I had a chance to convince him that I wasn't a threat. I had no doubt that Py would vouch for me, and maybe the footage from Doug and statements from the crew would help my case, too. Volunteering for work with the delegation in whatever capacity they could use me might help as well. That I was meeting the prince at all had to mean I had a chance, right?

Without thinking, I blurted out, "Am I still a suspect?"

Py looked up and stopped so suddenly that I nearly walked right into him. As it was, his tail ended up between my legs, making me dance backward to free it. Everyone was looking at me once I stood still, and I blushed brightly.

After a glance at the ensign, Py said to me, "No, you're not."

"Oh. Thank you."

Py gestured at me. "Ensign, please remove the tracker from him, and then let the duty sergeant know I'm canceling my order for an escort."

"Yes, sir." Ensign Codisin gave me a grin as they used a little key-like device to pop the lock on my tracking device. It gave a resigned beep and dropped into their hand. It had felt like I'd been wearing a watch and now I rubbed the blank spot. With another smile, the ensign walked away. Would I ever see them again?

And it was then that I realized I'd been so enmeshed in my worrying thoughts that I'd missed the fact that Py and I were alone in the hallway. "Sorry about that," I said to him. "I was...thinking," but I made a spiraling gesture with my hand.

He caught my hand and held it as he turned around to keep walking. "You aren't a suspect and no one will question your loyalties. Your interview aired moments before you arrived in my office, so I assume the prince and his mate have seen it by now."

I cringed. "So you haven't seen it yet?"

"No." He briefly squeezed my hand. "I won't if you would prefer that I didn't."

"You know the most painful parts, so I guess you can if you want to."

His thumb rubbed back and forth across my knuckles as we passed through a guarded doorway. The two... Dammit, what were the lizard-like Norlons called? I couldn't remember, but they were dressed in uniforms that looked more combat-ready. They didn't even glance at us as we passed, which made me feel like I really was in the clear.

Walking a little taller, I stuck by Py's side as we approached a door. Py touched a panel that beeped at him, and a moment later the door slid open. I'd been expecting opulence, but the prince's quarters weren't any fancier than Py's.

Py handled the introductions, and I was surprised when the prince reached for my hand.

"Please know that you have my condolences for the loss of your father."

I blinked up at him as he held my hand in both of his and gazed back at me with such sympathy in his bright blue eyes. Was he really separating the person from their acts? It felt like forgiveness and acceptance and maybe especially permission to mourn my father despite what he'd done. He'd been a good man once. A good father. Tears gathered and I had to look away as I nodded in thanks.

Logan put his hand on my back and said, "How about we get a drink, and then I can find a way to exploit your talents?"

His grin made me smile back. "Yeah, okay."

Py and the prince went over to a table and talked in low voices, while I followed Logan over to a small bar.

"So, Owen, do you want one drink that will knock your socks off, or a few that'll define the word mellow?"

I huffed a laugh. "Let's go with mellow. I could use some of that."

"I hear ya."

While he got glasses and poured a subtly pink liquid from a pitcher, I realized there was a hint of sex in the air. Was that me? My face exploded with heat as I tried to sniff without being obvious about it. We should've gone back to Py's quarters and showered. How embarrassing! I'd have to keep my distance from Logan so he wouldn't notice. Oh my god, did the wolf-looking prince have a better sense of smell? We were doomed.

"Let's have a seat," Logan said as he handed me my glass.

I followed him over to a pair of plush black chairs and sat down, hoping he couldn't tell I was a slut.

"Can I ask you something personal?" Logan whispered.

I stared at him with concern and nodded.

He glanced at our Norlons before looking again at me. "Does it smell like sex in here?"

I gasped in horror. "I'm *so sorry*. We should've showered first." I covered my mouth for a second. "I didn't even notice until a minute ago."

Logan laughed. "Oh, shit, I meant because that's what *we* were doing before you got here!"

I stared at him with my mouth hanging open. It wasn't just me?

"Okay, so…" He snickered and sipped his drink. "Never mind then. Alam was running around setting the air filters on high, but I guess he didn't need to worry about it."

My face didn't stop flaming, but relief washed through me. "Well, it's subtle which is why I thought it might be me. Those cleaning cloths can only do so much, you know?"

Logan snorted, and then suddenly we were both giggling like little kids. I was glad to know I wasn't the only one addicted to a Norlon to the point of doing dumb things when I shouldn't. I also laughed thinking that the captain of the ship and a prince of their people were setting one hell of an example for everyone else.

Py looked over, one eyebrow raised curiously, and I winked at him. He grinned at me and returned to talking with the prince. His pleased attention put a warmth in my chest and made me sigh.

"You've got it bad, too, huh?"

I looked to Logan, confused. "Got what?"

He hooked a thumb over his shoulder. "Him. Captain Tight-pants. I made Alam wait over a week, but he could've had me in a day if I hadn't been stupid."

My blush returned, but I wasn't completely embarrassed to have given in to the temptation of Py in less than twenty-four hours. "As bad as things have been," I said quietly, "he's the best person I've ever known."

Logan leaned over and gave my arm a squeeze. "You have my condolences, too, by the way. For your dad."

"Thanks." I sipped my drink.

"Are you going to the funeral this afternoon?"

"Oh, um, I didn't know about that."

He winced a bit. "Sorry to spring it on you. That's why the captain's here now. They're discussing their parts in it. Mostly, the funerals are for the Norlons who died, but they're going to include everyone." Logan shifted in his seat. "Then afterward, they'll be sending the deceased humans back to Earth. And anyone else who wants to go, too."

Which wasn't me. Even though my father would be going, I knew right away that I didn't want to go with him. It was probably my duty, there would no doubt be a funeral for him on the surface, and I knew several someone's would make note of my absence—but I wasn't going to go. I could mourn what could've been between us and the good memories I had, find some kind of closure, but it wouldn't be down there. At the moment, it felt like leaving heaven for hell.

"Yeah, I'll go to the funeral up here."

Logan seemed to get my meaning and nodded. "So, Alam said you might be interested in joining the delegation."

I was glad for the subject change and shifted in my seat to give him more of my attention. "If there's something I can help with, I'm happy to join up. I was pre-law and worked on my father's campaigns for a few summers in high school. Obviously, I'm not advocating for his conservative agenda or anything, but I know how those people work."

"And you know what language will and won't work for

them." Logan grinned at me. "You're like a double agent in a way."

I huffed a laugh. "I guess I *can* speak conservative. I'd be happy to help with that, even though it often makes me want to gag."

Logan nearly spit out a mouthful of his drink, gulping and choking as he chuckled. That he cut his eyes over to the prince, made me wonder if Logan was thinking about other things he could gag on. Which made me glance at Py and start blushing all over again.

When Logan was finally able to clear his throat, he said, "Welcome to the team, Owen. I think you're going to fit in perfectly."

I smiled and thanked him, already feeling like it was a team I could fight for.

CHAPTER 11
PYSINA

Though I was far from the spiritual leader on the ship, hearing my thoughts had seemed to offer some comfort to those who had attended the funeral for our fallen comrades. It didn't matter how many of these I attended throughout my career, I couldn't bounce back from the depression as quickly as my responsibilities required. With so many of my crew seasoned warriors or green recruits, I was certain I wasn't the only one struggling with the losses. I put the entire ship on minimum functions for the next twenty-four hours, with essential crew working only two-hour shifts at a time. Hopefully, that would help everyone.

Owen had attended the funeral with Logan, and I'd been glad that they were getting along so well. When I had watched the two of them leave with the prince's entourage, it was the first time that I didn't dread letting Owen out of my sight. Because I knew he was mine? Because I had claimed him in every way I could?

And yet I wasn't entirely sure he *was* mine.

Would he want to take his father's remains—what little

there was—down to the surface? I didn't doubt that that staff chief he had mentioned would make things difficult for Owen. Possibly to the point of taking over in every way. I wasn't versed in how human's mourned, but surely a son had duties or at least societal expectations where a deceased parent was concerned. The division between Owen and those loyal to his father probably meant a fight would await him on the ground.

I would have to be supportive if Owen chose to go. I couldn't go with him—my presence would only exacerbate the conflicts—but I would make sure he knew I'd wait for him.

Goddess, I didn't want him to go.

It turned out that I wasn't entirely at ease with his absence as I retreated to my quarters. I wasn't snarling in possessive pursuit of him, but I wasn't completely comfortable either. As I changed into a thick robe and prepared some tea, I considered and dismissed asking security to look for Owen. He could still be with Logan—hopefully, he was—because he didn't know his way around the ship. Yet he was also a grown man, and I shouldn't hover over him.

The door suddenly signaled, and I leapt over a chair to reach it.

Owen smiled slightly as he looked up at me. "Nice robe. Can I come in?"

"Of course." I stepped back to make room for him. "My quarters are yours…unless you would prefer to have your own."

He shook his head as he stepped out of his shoes and wiggled his little toes in the sitting area rug. "I want to stay here."

Tension eased from my shoulders, and I went to get him a cup of tea as well. "How did you find your way back?"

"Logan brought me."

I looked to the door, horrified that I hadn't even noticed the prince-consort.

Owen chuckled. "Don't worry. He predicted that you wouldn't know he was there once you saw me."

And Owen liked knowing he had every ounce of my attention. His smile and the twinkle in his eyes melted my heart. I brought the tea over to the sitting area and sat down to pour only to have him sit on my lap and snuggle in. I wrapped my arms around him and rested my chin on top of his head. The tea could steep a while longer.

The minutes ticked by as his warmth seeped into me before he whispered, "I don't want to go back to Earth."

I closed my eyes and swallowed hard, relief pouring through me. "Then you don't have to go."

"Don't I? Shouldn't I see him returned, plan a funeral, be the one everyone offers their condolences…to…" He trailed off as though having a new thought, and I waited. When he sat up, he was frowning as he said, "Who would even come to his funeral? They'd be making a statement of support, right? They'd be saying they were in favor of Humans First using bombs to kill people."

"Would they?" I had to ask. "Couldn't they simply mourn him? Offer their condolences to you for the loss of your father the same as the prince did?"

He glanced away, still frowning. "Privately, yeah, but not publicly. I mean, it would be great if they could, but we're talking about political leaders, influencers, donors… They're all either doubling down or distancing themselves after what he did." His face broke into an enormous smile. "This is going to be the big talking point for the next election. And that's just a few months away!"

His enthusiasm was the only thing I understood about any of that, so I smiled and asked, "Is this something that would help the delegation?"

Owen snuggled back against me with a wicked chuckle. "I'm going to mobilize the Rebel forces and shame the Imperialists by exploiting Vader's death."

Now I was the one frowning. "What?"

He giggled as he lifted his head to kiss me briefly. "I'm going to rile up those on our side and make everyone else look like villains for going against us." He thrust a fist into the air. "To the resistance!"

While his references were ever so confusing, I did understand his zeal to inspire or change minds as necessary. Seeing the flush of his cheeks and spark in his eyes had me pulling him in for a deeper kiss this time. Owen's little moan and the way he opened for me, his fingers combing through the fur of my cheek, began to wipe away the gloom within me.

Pulling back, he peered at me. "Are you okay?" he asked quietly.

I shrugged one shoulder and offered a small smile, not sure if I wanted to talk about loss with him.

Owen nodded. "You've probably been to a lot of funerals."

"I have."

He gently scratched at my jaw, sending a shiver through me. "How can I help?"

I smiled more genuinely. "You already are."

Shifting back, he stood up from my lap and reached out a hand. I clasped it without hesitation.

"How about a massage?" he suggested. "Take off the robe and lay face down on the bed."

I'd had plenty of professional massages but that I would be naked for this one and Owen would be the one touching me had my cock perking up before I'd fully removed my robe. Biting his bottom lip, Owen took off his tunic, leaving his lower body wrapped in tight dark blue cloth that hid nothing. He waved me toward the bed, so I lay down as instructed.

He started at my feet. I couldn't see him, but his touches seemed to say that he was fascinated by the pads of my toes and the spaces in between. Involuntarily, I flexed and shivered as he explored. He was soon working his way up my legs, massaging muscles and sifting through fur. When he reached my thighs, I spread them wider and lifted my tail in invitation.

Owen's quiet chuckle sounded wicked as he rubbed my ass muscles. He made me gasp when his thumbs pulled my cheeks apart, exposing my hole. I hadn't let a lover inside me since I was young—my preferences clear from an early age—but I was tempted as Owen climbed onto the bed and paused to grind himself against me. He giggled, though, like he was only teasing, and I groaned in anticipation of being allowed to turn over and take him.

His firm massaging of my lower back did actually alleviate some tension there, which I appreciated almost as much as the erotic sensations he was causing. He continued to dig his little fingers into the muscles of my back and all the way up to my shoulders. That his hard cock rode the valley of my spine didn't seem to steal his focus as much as it did mine. Goddess bless, he was tempting me to flip over and plow him into the floor.

"Turn over," he whispered into my ear, and I groaned in thanks.

While he went to get the lubricant, I rolled onto my back, curious to see what he intended now. Was he simply preparing and would now massage the front of me? Would he slick my cock and ride me, controlling the ride?

Owen got back on the bed and straddled my thighs, my cock upthrust directly in front of him. With a grin on his lips, he used one finger to tease the protrusion at the head of my cock and make me gasp. He giggled as he opened the lube.

But then he made a little growling noise as he seemed to realize he'd have to get down to remove his pants. Since my claws were already out, I reached between his legs and set one claw to the seam of his pants. They made an obscene sound as I tore through the threads, the tight material parting immediately to free his cock and balls and open the way to his delectable ass.

Owen gasped as though scandalized, and I chuckled at him. I touched his hole with the pad of my finger to hear him gasp again before putting my hands behind my head. He blinked at me a few times as I grinned.

"Well, alright," he said and wiggled into position. "Destructive, but convenient."

I was about to say some quip, but he stole my thoughts away as he slicked my cock. He played, taking his time, driving me insane with need. I reached down to grasp his thighs, and he gave me a cocky grin. Shifting forward, he aimed me at his hole and then slowly bounced on my cock, taking me deeper with each downward plunge. All I could do was watch him ride me, his head thrown back and eyes closed as he gave himself over to the sensations of being filled.

Goddess, he was beautiful. For a long while, I could only stare at him and feel his thigh muscles flex under my hands as he moved up and down. No one compared to my Owen. No one ever would.

But Owen's sensuous pace was going to kill me. Grabbing

his waist, I flipped us over and immediately drove my cock deep into him. He hollered and gripped my shoulders, his legs wrapping around my waist. Face flushed and big eyes staring up at me, I grinned as I pounded into him.

"Yes, yes, yes," he chanted. "Take me. Claim me!"

Remembering how he'd needed to know he was mine, I dipped my head and set my teeth to the juncture of his neck and shoulder. He wailed and his already tight ass squeezed on me as his fingers bit into my shoulders. Inside, I smiled to know he might leave claiming bruises on me, too.

When I had him whining and thrusting up to meet me, I growled low in my throat. He went quiet and still before his entire body tensed and he came with a yell. I couldn't resist the way his body pulled me in and I lifted my head to holler my own release, filling him, marking him inside and out.

Once I had my breath back, I stepped away, pleased to see him sprawled and relaxed on my bed. Since I had been taking him with frequency, I'd procured a salve with nanobots in it that would assist in making certain he didn't suffer. Claws retracted, I gently eased a daub of the salve inside him, being sure to coat his rim as well.

"What's that?" He lifted his head just before he gasped and his eyes went wide. "It tingles."

"I've already taken you once today, so this should help you recover."

He gave a breathy moan as I continued to spread the salve. I didn't need to, it was working already, but since I was there…

"Ugh, Py," he said on a whine, "you're going to get me hard again."

I licked a stripe up his flushed cock, making him holler. Continuing to finger his ass, I sucked his semi-hard cock into my mouth and teased his delicate balls with my other hand. He writhed against the bedding, his hands crushing it in his fists, while he made the most obscenely beautiful sounds of pleasure. It wasn't long before he came again, whimpering and shivering.

Getting back on the bed, I pulled him into my arms and threw a leg over his. He moaned into my neck, fingers gripping my fur as if I might not hold him close for the rest of my life.

"You're mine," I whispered.

He took a deep breath and sighed, nodding.

CHAPTER 12
OWEN

Was it possible to be in a honeymoon phase while in a brand-new relationship? Technically, I was living with Py, so I figured we were officially official. He'd introduced me as his mate to some of his commanders a couple days ago, too. Everything felt fluffy and sunshiny. Py would spend every evening with me as long as he wasn't needed somewhere else. We'd had dinner out a couple of times and even gone to see a movie once. And our nights… Woo! We were going through gallons of lube and that nanobot salve let me keep up with Py's insatiable libido.

Yet somewhere in the back of my mind, I kept waiting for the bad thing to happen. This kind of bliss couldn't possibly last. Surely, I would screw it up eventually simply because I was so inexperienced. I had no idea what I was doing, how to be in a relationship, or whether I was doing things right. I *was* happy. I thought Py was happy, too. But was that enough?

That fear was probably what drove me to be indispensable to the delegation. Like if there were things I excelled at, my value to others would increase. Which kind of made me sound a little pathetic but didn't stop me from volunteering for whatever popped up.

Though, I should've probably double-checked what sort of documentary we would be screening *before* I walked into the conference room.

"We haven't finalized the title yet," Administrator Ghosha Progoni Rijal said at the front of the room, "so that's something this group could assist with, as well as your impressions of how the humans of Earth will receive the information."

He was a large muscular tiger-like alien who could've been intimidating just from his appearance alone, but it was clear even to me that he was nervous. And no wonder! It was the first screening of a documentary about a day in the life of a human sex worker in a brothel on Nor, for heaven's sake. As the unofficial interpreter of conservative America, I already knew there would be protests and accusations the second they found out about this. I cringed just thinking imagining it.

But I stayed in my seat and paid attention as several other humans and even more Norlons watched the ninety-minute movie with me. None of the interviewees had sex on screen, but the star discussed it several times. I thought everything was tasteful, honest, and informative, just well done in every way, but dear god, I knew the film would be seen as grooming and recruitment by every right-wing zealot out there. Rijal might as well have made a porn film because they'd see it as the same thing.

Well, actually no, they'd never *see* the documentary. They'd just pretend they had and scream about it like they did with everything else they didn't agree with. No active learning for them!

What I learned, though, was that I definitely wasn't the only human man fascinated by a slightly aggressive, wildly furry, and deliciously well-hung Norlon. Hearing Korey talk about his male and female Norlon clients reminded me of every sexual escapade I'd had with Py. It was entirely possible that a sex worker had taught a young Py everything he knew and did with me.

Honestly, if I didn't have Py, I might've signed up for a one-way ticket into Nor's thriving sex industry after watching this movie.

Well, I might've been able to *imagine* doing it. Vividly, but… Yeah, just in my head.

Py was it for me.

As the credits started rolling, the lights came back on, and Administrator Rijal walked to the front of the room again. He was wringing his hands as he gazed out at us, the poor guy. Wanting to boost his spirits since all of this was going to be hard enough, I started clapping. My fellow humans quickly took up the cause, and then the Norlons joined in. Rijal huffed a laugh and grinned as he bowed to us.

What followed was a sort of Q and A, where he'd ask a question and we'd answer. I didn't know about distribution methods, but agreed with putting it online to maximize the number of people who could see it—they didn't want to profit or let others profit and so wanted to keep it out of theaters. With age restrictions in place, they could limit the audience appropriately while still making it accessible.

When the discussion shifted to the film's reception down on Earth, several heads turned my way, though I bet most of them knew what I'd have to say.

"Well, um," I said as I stood up. "There will be backlash, like there's been for everything else. You'll have people claiming you're grooming children, promoting a gay agenda, encouraging sex trafficking… Being able to counter those points intelligently and calmly will be important, especially in the beginning."

"Can you help with that?" Rijal asked. "The counter points?"

"Oh, sure, of course." Looked like I had some homework. "Could I get a copy so I can make notes?"

"Layleen will make sure there's a copy on your tablet," he said, gesturing to a long-eared gray Pip.

"Great. Thanks." I nodded to both of them and sat back down.

After the session ended, several of us went over and offered encouragement to Rijal and his team. They seemed to appreciate it.

Logan walked with me as we left, surprising me because I hadn't thought I'd see him today. "Man, I feel bad for them," he said.

"Yeah, they're the one mission that's never going to have an easy time of anything."

"They don't quit, though."

"Right? That takes a lot of inner strength." I paused at a split in the hallway, squinting down the left side because I felt like that was the way I wanted to go, which probably meant it was wrong.

Logan chuckled at me. "Where are you heading?"

"My quarters. I'm going to get started on my notes."

He pointed to the right. I sighed and walked along with him, glad my instinct to ignore my instincts was getting better.

"While I was watching," Logan said, "I couldn't help thinking that sex work seemed so reasonable. Like why can't we just make it a legitimate career choice?"

"I thought the same thing! Because if we had a real and

honest relationship with sex, maybe other things like our sexual identities wouldn't be so controversial. I mean, if being gay was just something you could put on a resume, then where's the problem?"

Logan practically moaned, the sound envious. "Goddamn, that would be amazing."

I bit my lip and hesitated before I made myself say, "Am I crazy to think that making this deal with Nor could change the world?"

He bumped my shoulder and grinned. "Nothing wrong with hoping."

We walked down another hallway, and I thought maybe it looked familiar. What I needed were more signs. Most of the rooms were really big on these levels, so if it was a conference room or something, there might only be a sign every fifty feet. And now that we were on a level of mostly personnel quarters, there weren't any signs, just labels like apartment numbers.

"Oh my gosh," I said as it suddenly occurred to me why I hadn't thought I'd see Logan around today. "Aren't you getting *married* tomorrow?"

"Yeah?" He looked genuinely confused by my outburst.

"But don't you have wedding things to be doing?"

Logan smirked at me. "Hon, I have a whole platoon of people working on wedding things. At this point, Alam and I just have to show up and look pretty."

"Oh. Sure, that makes sense." He was royalty, after all. "Are you nervous?"

"Nah," he said with a cute grin. "By Norlon standards, we're already in a committed relationship that's the equivalent of being married. There's a mating ceremony we'll do for his people and family when we go to Nor, but it's nothing as fancy as what you and I know a wedding can be."

"Then I guess the prince isn't nervous at all."

Logan laughed. "He's terrified he's going to forget his vows! He keeps practicing in the bathroom because he thinks I can't hear him in there. Even *I've* memorized his vows at this point."

"Aw, that's adorable! Both that he's trying so hard and that he wrote vows." I could feel the hearts in my eyes even as I laughed with Logan.

"And Captain Langarus is going to officiate," he said, "which meant explaining what that's all about. But how can I pass up the opportunity to be married by a spaceship's captain?"

I chuckled with him since that was so true. Married at sea sounded romantic enough, but married in space? With aliens? I pressed a hand over my heart just as I realized Logan had led me to my quarters.

We said goodbye, and I wished him luck for tomorrow. When the door opened, I smiled upon seeing that Py was inside. He sat watching a wedding video with his tablet in his hand like he might be taking notes.

"Are you nervous about tomorrow, too?" I went over to try to get a peek at his tablet.

"I have lines I must memorize." He angled the tablet so I could see that he'd written out the usual lines an officiant would say. "I discovered a great deal of controversy surrounding whether or not to include obeying one's new spouse, though."

"Oh, yeah, leave that off. It's really outdated and from when women were treated as property."

His eyes widened. "They were property?"

"Um, well, humans have a messed up history of doing that. The strong owning the weak. I'd love to say we're over it now, but some attitudes persist." I blinked and stared at nothing as something suddenly occurred to me. "You know, it's possible a lot of what's fueling stuff like Humans First comes from people being afraid that they're the weak ones now. They used to believe they were the strong ones and know how they treated everyone else. They're afraid that's how they'll be treated."

"They would deserve it for such atrocities, but overtaking humans and owning them is not our goal."

"Oh, I know." I squeezed his shoulder and went to sit down. "They're not being rational."

Py spent a few moments changing things on his tablet, possibly erasing notes on obeying. Since he was here—playing hooky from captaining?—I took advantage of his knowledge while I had him. "What's a mating ceremony like?"

He looked me in the eyes and then glanced at his notes before shrugging. "Similar to this, though no one leads like I must. Promises are made and tokens exchanged. In the case of royals, someone might announce where territories will merge or what resources will be shared going forward."

I wrinkled my nose. "Seems a little business-like."

"It is the business of being mated."

"Oh." That was disappointing.

"The party afterward is the celebration."

"Oh?"

Py smirked at me. "Games, wagers, and orgies are common."

"I-I'm sorry. Did you say…orgies?"

"I did."

"But, um, I thought having a mate was a monogamous thing."

"It is. Often the mated couple will be unable to resist staking their claims on each other and that will inspire their audience to experience the same joys."

A bark of a laugh jumped out of me and I blushed. Could that happen tomorrow? The Norlons might be inspired, but the humans from Earth were still here and the news crew might end up filming everything. Hopefully it wouldn't be a live broadcast.

Py chuckled. "It's voluntary, Owen."

"Oh, sure. No, I get it." I squirmed in my seat.

"If inspiration strikes," he said with a wicked grin, "we could find a darkened alcove or just return here."

We could, could we? I suddenly knew what was going to rule my brain for the next twenty-four hours.

CHAPTER 13
PYSINA

Indulging the prince-consort's wishes by officiating his wedding was no hardship and that it clearly delighted the royal couple pleased me as well. My fellow Norlons were polite and reserved as befitted a royal mating ceremony, despite the script not calling for their involvement in supporting the new couple. On the whole, though, it was a nice service that left everyone smiling as we changed venues from the spiritual center to the garden deck with a clear view of Earth.

Well, everyone was smiling except Owen. He'd waited for me as everyone filed out into the corridors, and I could easily scent his nervousness as I joined him. When I took his hand, he gripped mine rather tightly. I knew he had no issues regarding sex with me, but I probably shouldn't have mentioned that orgies were common during the celebration after the ceremony. Owen had been twitchy ever since.

"We can make an appearance," I said quietly as we walked, "and congratulate the prince and prince-consort before we leave. Staying isn't required."

"Oh, no, I want to go to the party." He looked up at me with concern. "Unless you don't?"

"You seem nervous."

He shrugged and his cheeks colored. "I was never a partier, so I've never done something wild or in public. This feels like anything could happen, and I don't know what I'll do when it does."

"Ah. Nervous excitement." I had to wonder if he was interested in allowing me to mate him, if that was one of the wild things that might happen.

"Well, yeah, I guess so. Because I've always wanted to experience stuff like this without the restrictions that have always been on me."

"Because of your father," I guessed.

"Right."

I gave his hand a squeeze. "Now you're free."

Owen smiled up at me as we entered the garden through an arch of twinkling lights.

The newly mated couple was on a dais, seated on thrones, and accepting well-wishes from the line of people ringing the walled side of the room. Many others held drinks and food and were gathered on the other side where a wall of tinted windows allowed views of Earth. Plants of all sorts grew from raised beds throughout the room and tiny lights were the only illumination. It was a lovely and intimate setting for a mating celebration.

I waited with Owen to congratulate the new couple, passing the time by answering as many of his questions as I could about the plants around us. I hadn't truly considered that Earth and Nor would have different flora, but it made sense that they would. Apparently, purple leaves and flowers as big as my head were rare and exotic on Earth, but I knew those plants had been chosen for the ship because they were so common on Nor that everyone would recognize them. The garden deck was meant to be a place of quiet contemplation and peace and so it was designed to be comforting.

"Hey, Owen," the prince-consort greeted warmly when we stood before them. "And Captain Langarus, you were awesome." He came down to hug us both.

"Thank you," I said. "It was an honor."

"The ceremony was *beautiful*," Owen gushed. "Prince Ye Lena, your vows were just…" He put a hand over his heart and made a little whining noise. "They were *perfect*."

The couple clasped hands and beamed at each other before the prince said, "Thank you. My words were from my heart."

Owen made another whimpering noise and leaned into me. He loved love, and I wrapped an arm around him as we took our leave so the next group could offer their thoughts to the couple.

I led Owen over to procure a glass of fedesmia from the prince's own family stock and enough food so that the effects of the drink wouldn't impair Owen too quickly. Music played through hidden speakers, the volume low for now and only instrumental.

"We're over Canada, right?" Owen asked as he gazed out the window.

"We are. As we both rotate into night, the windows will darken to ease the brightness of the sun. Soon the only light in here will be the ones hidden amongst the plants."

He looked me in the eyes and a blush crept over his cheeks as he grinned, letting me know he understood why I'd mentioned any of that. Not long from now, as everyone relaxed, inhibitions would fall away and many would take advantage of the darkness. Would Owen?

I hoped he would. I wanted him to have every freedom denied him in his old life. If he wanted to dance and drink and gamble, I would do my best to keep up and fund his fun. But most of all, if he wanted to allow me to claim him in front of all of these people, I would do my utmost to give him his every desire.

Once the greetings concluded, the music volume increased and dancing began. Gaming tables came out and the hollers of winners and losers rang through the room. Owen was terrible at gambling, but he had so much fun trying that I didn't mind continuing to put up credits. Plus, whatever we lost would fund donations to the injured and the families of those lost in the explosion, so I was doubly happy to provide.

As the darkness grew and drinks flowed, I began to notice several guests indulging in sexual activities with each other. Even some of the visiting humans were scattered about and kissing Norlons, many hands roaming. I didn't worry about them, but did look down at Owen to see if he'd realized what was happening around him.

Drink halfway to his lips, mouth open, and eyes wide, Owen stared into the room at the many writhing bodies. He was blushing as I moved around behind him. I pressed my lips to his ear as I whispered, "Mating celebrations often inspire orgies, remember?"

OWEN

I gasped and twitched in Py's embrace as I gazed out at the scene. Of course I remembered what he'd said yesterday about the mating celebration inspiring orgies amongst the guests. I just hadn't expected to actually witness it. Like I thought they might not do it since it we weren't on Nor or because there were so many humans who'd never been to one of these events before. And they were definitely starting to notice.

"I don't want to be with anyone but you," I whispered to him as I set my drink down.

"Then you won't be." He took a deep breath through his nose. "Still, this inspires you."

It did. Damn, did it inspire me.

"Shall I take you home?" His tongue gave my cheek a tiny lick.

I shivered, but… Inside I groaned because I didn't want to leave. I'd never in my life gone to a frat party or a club because I'd always had to be on my best behavior. There couldn't be photos of me drinking or dancing or doing anything that would've given me away to people who would've used me against my father's political aspirations. But right now, I was at the party and I could drink and dance and…fuck my boyfriend.

Biting my bottom lip and blushing ferociously, I shook my head.

Py pressed his cheek to mine, and I felt him grin. "Should I hide under the nearest table and suck you off? No one would see me, but they would see you."

"T-tempting."

"Reverse it then. You hide."

"I'd miss everything."

His rumbling laugh vibrated through me. "We could do as our hosts are," he said with a nod toward the main table.

I gasped as I realized Logan was sitting on the prince's lap.

Well, not just his lap if the glorious agony on Logan's face was anything to go by. My guess was that there was a very big cock up his ass and maybe a knot, too. They were being discreet—the only tell-tale sign being the way Logan was rocking his hips—and it was still sexy as hell.

"I, um… I do want…that."

Py's hand slithered down my abs and then he was cupping me through my tunic and pants. My hips jerked, shoving my erection into his palm. I felt the faintest prick of his claws and couldn't help a tiny whimper.

"We're in the back of the room, and everyone's attention is on themselves." He nuzzled my neck briefly, stealing another lick. "Raise your tunic and push your pants down just a bit. I'll take care of everything else and it's possible no one will ever know."

But I'd know. I'd never forget it.

Panting from anticipation and amazement at my own boldness, I reached down and lifted my red and gold tunic up to my lower back. With Py plastered to me, we held the thick fabric in place. I stopped staring at Logan and the prince and started glancing around at everyone else, making sure no one was looking this way.

"I could tear the seam," Py offered like the devil he was.

I took a shaky breath and nodded.

He eased a hand between us, and I felt every thread snap as his single claw broke it. Cool air touched the crack of my ass, sending a shiver of stark, wanton need cascading over me. I tried to slow my breathing, calm my heart, as Py looped one arm around me, making very sure I wasn't going anywhere.

Suddenly, the wet head of his cock and that stiff little protrusion kissed my hole and made me gasp. Open-mouthed, I blinked at the gyrating crowd as Py thrust his way into me. I could't stop myself from moaning. No one looked over. No one noticed. They were too caught up in what they were doing and feeling to care that my mate was claiming me.

But I cared. I wanted them to look and know who I belonged to. Who belonged to me.

I clutched at Py's arm and couldn't help my noises as he filled me and withdrew with a perfectly maddening pace. My eyes rolled closed when he set his teeth against the join of my neck and shoulder, just resting there for now. I reached up and got a handful of the soft fur at his cheek, determined to keep him on me, and went up on my toes to get his dick deeper into me.

"Py," I whined over how slow he was going. I could feel every vein in his cock and the bulge of his knot as it glided inside my stretched open ass. "*Please.*"

He braced a hand against the jut of the wall beside us and then really railed me. I couldn't hear the slap of our bodies but I swore he matched the beat of the music on purpose. And it was dance music, fast and pounding. Py was thrusting like a piston, and I could barely catch my breath as my orgasm sped up on me.

For just a second, I tried to resist out of fear that someone would see or a flash would go off. But then Py bit me and I came with a holler of pure bliss, my eyes closed and my mind not giving a shit who saw this beautiful moment of wicked perfection between me and the fox I loved.

With Py's knot grinding on my prostate in sharp ecstasy, I felt him growl around his mouthful of me before he punched his hips forward and came. My breath caught and I wasn't sure if I was still coming or coming again.

When he lifted his head, I opened my eyes and actually smiled when I made eye contact with Doug, the PBS News anchor. He stood not far away with both hands stroking the head of the Khess on their knees in front of him. He grinned at me, and I grinned back.

People saw. They knew.

Py straightened out my tunic and then took my hand. While it wasn't the most comfortable walk back to our quarters, I kept right on grinning the entire way there. Freedom felt incredible.

CHAPTER 14
OWEN

"Ready?" Ghosha glanced at me sitting across the table from him. I nodded and offered the best smile I had available. He checked with everyone else, and then he connected the call.

We were in one of the smaller conference rooms on the ship and about to make the first of several video conference calls with politicians on the surface who had concerns about the sex work volunteers. I was the only human in the room and my purpose was to talk down any right wingers who might get loud. I'd coached everyone on what may happen, armed them as best I could, but it was understood that I'd step in if things got bad. To say that I was nervous would be… Well, I'd already thrown up once.

The man who'd served as lieutenant governor under my father, Don Musted, would be among the callers as the new governor of Ohio. He wasn't a better choice in any way at all, and he was the reason my stomach was in knots. While Brett could spin his hate and make it sound sweet, Musted wouldn't hesitate to spew his vitriol, especially not now that he was in charge.

When his face appeared on my tablet with the rest of them, I couldn't help gulping.

"What's *he* doing here?" Musted sneered.

Across from me, Ghosha asked, "To whom are you referring?"

"Don't get high and mighty with me. What's that traitor doing on this call?"

Oh. He meant me. I cleared my throat and tried to smile. "Hello, Governor Musted. I'm here to help—"

"I want him off this call immediately and out of that room."

I looked questioningly at Ghosha. I honestly hadn't thought he'd demand that. Should I leave?

Ghosha barely shook his head before saying, "Owen is a member of the delegation tasked with—"

"I don't care! You people can do whatever you like with him up there, but he's not going to be involved with anything attached to *my name*."

Good grief, the ego on him. And something about it all tripped a switch inside me that completely wiped out my nervousness and replaced it with a feeling that was a lot more useful. I smiled genuinely and said, "It's alright, Governor, I'll go. But before I do, I'd love to know if your stepdaughter Brigit had her baby. Is it a boy or a girl? I'd love to send a gift."

Months ago, I'd heard my father telling Brett that Musted had drunkenly confessed to being the father of Brigit's baby and that she was blackmailing him to keep her silence. I hadn't been completely surprised since my one meeting with her had made it clear she was in it to win by any means necessary. They all deserved each other, and I desperately hoped the baby would be put up for adoption to save the little innocent from them.

I watched in devious delight as Musted's face paled and sweat broke out on his forehead. The silence was deafening as everyone on the call and in the room waited for him to respond. Though he didn't move a muscle, someone on his end must've ended his call because he was gone a moment later.

Now it was Ghosha who raised a furry white eyebrow as he held my gaze. I tried to look innocent and said for the benefit of everyone else, "Oh dear. I hope Brigit and the baby are alright. I didn't mean to touch a nerve."

Others mentioned their concerns as well since Brigit had all but disappeared from the public in the last few months, no one having known she was pregnant. I tried very hard not to grin.

After that, the conversation was a lot more productive. While not everyone was of the opinion that sex work could be a viable career option, at least no one got nasty. It turned out to be a pretty good debate that boiled down to free will. Sex work might be illegal in the US, but that didn't mean the government could stop a citizen from leaving the country to do such work somewhere that it was legal. I was oddly proud that we got to that point with these politicians. When Ghosha ended the call, we were all smiling in triumph.

We did a wrap-up, adding free will to our arsenal of talking points, and someone asked if making these sessions public would help our cause. I let them know that recording and distributing the call would have to be known ahead of time by all participants, but that it wasn't unusual to upload videos of such things somewhere for the public to view. I had a feeling the Norlons would have a YouTube channel connected to their website before the end of the day.

Just as we were breaking for lunch, I got a note from Py

about the visiting humans getting ready to leave. Through him, I'd known the shuttle bay repairs had been completed yesterday and had wondered if that would be the kickoff to everyone going back to the surface. They hadn't needed to wait since shuttles were docked all over the ship, and it had been great having the news crew here, especially because they'd been doing regular broadcasts. I had to assume that they felt they'd been away from their families and lives long enough if they were leaving now, though.

Doug had never mentioned what either of us had done during the mating celebration, but he'd sometimes wink at me, making me blush.

Since I wanted to say good-bye to him and everyone else with PBS, I rushed off toward the shuttle bay. Py had put a map of the ship on my tablet that acted like a navigation app, so I was finally able to get around on my own. Several hallways and two lifts later, I walked into the bay.

Py always looked so stately and scrumptious in his uniform. Today's short red coat emphasized his broad shoulders and trim waist, while the tight black pants left absolutely nothing to the imagination. His bushy orange and white tail was up and still, making me think he was alert to his surroundings. One tall ear swiveled around just before he looked over his shoulder at me and grinned.

I went over to stand beside him, and he took my hand in his. He was so sweet.

"How was your meeting?" he asked.

"Good. Really good, actually. I'll tell you what I did when we're alone."

He gave my hand a squeeze before people started arriving and others came over to say good-bye.

Doug hugged the stuffing out of me, and his producer

Ashley said all I needed to do was call and I could be on the air in minutes. That was pretty amazing, and I agreed that I wouldn't hesitate if necessary.

When everyone was onboard and the crew was finishing up preparations, Py cleared his throat and gave me a sideways look that I thought seemed nervous. "I should have told you this sooner, so please forgive me that I didn't."

I took his hand again. "What's wrong?"

He shook his head. "It's not wrong, just information you probably should have known before now." He leveled a golden stare at me. "Owen, I am a ship's captain. For the rest of my career, I will be on a ship. Whether it's this one and orbiting here, or others on different missions, I will rarely be on land for many years to come."

I nodded up at him. Sure, I hadn't really given the details of his job much thought, but I hadn't assumed he'd be quitting any time soon.

"It doesn't bother you?" he asked. "You would stay with me?"

I gasped, realizing he'd been worried I wouldn't like being on a ship for years and years. "Oh, Py, no! It doesn't bother me and of course I'll stay." I kissed his knuckles and cuddled his hand between us. "I'm happy to ride around on a spaceship with my mate."

I could see him relax as a little smile lifted his dark lips. He pulled my hand up so he could kiss my knuckles in return, and I tucked in a bit closer to him.

"Forgive me," he said. "You're my first mate, and I wonder sometimes if I'm doing things right."

I clicked my tongue at him. "Well, you're my first anything, and I think we're doing fine."

He cocked his head at me and blinked kind of slowly, like a question.

"I mean, I used plenty of toys before," I explained, blushing. "*Plenty* of them. But, um, you're the first person to ever be, you know, inside me. That's significant for me."

Py stared at me long enough for me to consider asking if he'd heard me, but then he nodded and looked back over at the departing shuttle. Well, that wasn't exactly the reaction I'd hoped for when revealing that I'd given him my virginity, but maybe this wasn't the place to discuss it? We weren't alone even if it was noisy enough to drown out our conversation.

When a tone sounded, I realized everyone working in the bay had started stepping out through various doors around the room. Py's hand suddenly gripped the back of my neck. "I have urgent business in the cargo bay."

"Oh, uh—" I tried to say before he swung me around and pushed me from the room.

We continued across the hall and into an enormous space filled with barrels bigger than me and giant plastic crates I could live inside. I hoped Py didn't mind that his manhandling of me was getting me hot because it really was. His claws were poking into my neck as he kept steering me through the stacks, deeper into the room. What could the captain of the ship need to do in here? Maybe we were meeting someone. Hopefully they wouldn't be able to scent my arousal.

Finally, we stopped and... Py pressed me face-first into a crate? I tried to look back at him, but then he kicked my feet farther apart. There was only one reason I could think of for him to do that and a shiver lit through me.

"Did you know I keep lube with me now because of you?" He let my neck go to ruck up my deep purple tunic to my waist. A second later and the seam of my black pants split open with the help of one of his wicked claws. "Being your first is very significant. Goddess, Owen," he practically moaned.

I couldn't help giggling as I leaned where I was and listened to him slick his dick with the lube he kept on him just for me. Apparently that nod he'd given me after learning he was my first hadn't been his only reaction—he'd just done a masterful job of keeping his passion contained.

Until now anyway. That Py couldn't wait for a more private location than deep in a cargo hold where anyone might find us was a huge compliment in my opinion.

I rested my crossed wrists on the crate above my head, and Py took the hint to grasp them there and hold on. Tipping my ass up, I bit my bottom lip as he painted the crack of my ass with the wet tip of his cock. My dick was filling fast, lifting the front of my tunic and making me shiver as it slid against the silky material.

"Please, Py, do it." There was a definite whine to my voice, but I couldn't help it. If he didn't hurry up, I might come from his teasing.

"Mine," he said as he finally eased into me.

The stretch stole my breath as he growled in my ear, making the sensations that much more powerful. He pressed his free hand against my lower belly, fingers splayed around the base of my dick, and held me still as he worked his way deeper into my ass. I couldn't help the desperate little noises leaving me as I closed my eyes and let him in.

I was up on my toes and panting by the time I felt his furry pelvis pressed to my cheeks, the whole of his glorious cock inside me. I could feel his claws pressing into my sensitive skin, some of them against my balls, and bumped back against him to try and make him move. But Py just hummed and rubbed his face against my head and neck like he was marking me.

"We fit together perfectly," he whispered.

I nodded. "We…we do."

He withdrew slowly, making me wail in pleasure. I wasn't sure, but it almost sounded like he chuckled.

"P-Py, I swear to god…"

His thrust back into me was faster, but he was definitely taking his time with this fuck, the bastard. I hung there, trapped between him and the crate, his claws teasing me, and utterly unable to do anything but twitch my ass and cry out for more. Goddamn, it was brilliantly devastating in the best ways.

When he finally lost his ability to go slowly, I could've wept in relief. His hips pistoned that marvelous dick of his in and out of me, his knot rubbing perfectly, until I was nothing but a mass of raw nerves desperate for release. I couldn't stop hollering, begging without words for him to finish me.

With one swipe of his hand over the length of my dick, I came with a yell and shot so hard onto the crate that it sounded like a hose unleashed. My knees buckled, but Py was ready for it and caught me against him with both arms around me. He fucked me a few more times before he had the audacity to come with a contented sigh, like he hadn't taken a decade to get us there. The little yip he gave right after had me grinning, though.

Tucked close together while we got our breaths back under control, Py whispered, "You're giving me a bad reputation. Six people have tried to work around us and fled instead."

I snorted. "I'm giving you a *fantastic* reputation. You're a sex god. Everyone's jealous."

He chuckled and pressed his cold nose to my cheek before giving me a lick.

We got ourselves presentable again... Well, no, we didn't. We looked and smelled like we'd fucked in a back room, but no one could tell my pants were split thanks to the length of my tunic. They could probably guess, of course, but they couldn't see it. We walked to our quarters holding hands.

"What was it you wanted to tell me about the meeting?" he asked.

"Oh, someone got mad that I was there," I said with a big smile, "so I scared the hell out of him and made him run away."

Py paused and cupped my cheek. "I'm so proud of you."

I was proud of me, too. It was kind of a gross thing to do, but I could fight fire with fire nowadays and wouldn't ever be afraid to stand up for myself again. And it was all thanks to the sexy fox captain who'd claimed me.

"I love you, Py. You're the best thing that's ever happened to me."

He gave me a little kiss. "You are my everything, and I love you, too."

THANK YOU FOR READING!

I sincerely hope you enjoyed reading Py and Owen's story as much as I loved writing it!

If you would be so kind as to write a review telling other readers why you liked this book, that would really help me. As an independent author, reviews are super important to my success.

Please leave your review for *Claimed by the Fox Captain* at Amazon.

For a sneak peek at Chapter 1 of the next book, *Bound to the Tiger Scout*, turn the page!

BOUND TO THE TIGER SCOUT
GHOSHA PROGONI RIJAL

CHAPTER 1

Unable to stand it one more second, I muted everyone on the shared call with the surface and smiled. "If I may? My name is Ghosha Progoni Rijal. You have my permission to call me Ghosha, but you can also maintain formality and use my title and family name to call me Administrator Rijal." I stopped smiling and said firmly, "I am not 'the tiger.'"

I gave the American politicians a moment to mull that over, only for three of them to immediately try to talk again. I sighed. Oh how I wished I had been better prepared for the prudishness of Earth humans. Those on Nor had said to expect some pushback, but they had also said things might have changed in the decades since they'd been gone from their home world.

I could confirm now that nothing had improved.

I unmuted everyone just in time to hear one of the humans call me a "fucking rude-ass beast" before she cut herself off with a gasp.

"And if I might also remind you," I said pleasantly, "this session is being recorded for public consumption this afternoon."

That, I had discovered, seemed to be the only way to keep polite the people I was forced to deal with on the topic of human sex workers. I was now releasing every single session I had on the website so that every human everywhere could see how their leaders were handling the negotiations. The media coverage was thorough and global, though the reactions were mixed.

If that didn't make these people act professionally, I was going to make the sessions live. Maybe invite the press to ask questions during the sessions, too.

"Now, if we might return to the topic at hand," I said as I laced my fingers and tried to smile. "You are unhappy with Americans volunteering for sex work?"

A month or so ago, the delegation had launched their website in order to control their message. One part of that had been explaining the basics, like the proper word to use for my people—I was a Khess—while other parts of the site had delved into deeper topics like the capabilities of nanobots and sex work as a respected career.

My focus was on asking for humans to volunteer to work in the brothels on Nor. There were only twenty-two humans who worked in the brothels now, and several of them were interested in retirement. Since many Norlons enjoyed sex with humans—and vice versa—the brothels had petitioned for an administrator amongst the delegation to take up their cause. The website, therefore, had a form detailing the expectations of sex workers on Nor, the benefits, and the requirements.

We had received over one hundred thousand applications in the first week.

And then the politicians began to protest.

Regardless of which country it was, their leaders had a long list of reasons why "their people" could absolutely not participate. While I could respect their traditions, religious requirements, or whatever else they mentioned, the fact that someone had cast off those things voluntarily in order to signup had to count for something as well. It had to mean more, didn't it? Norlons believed wholeheartedly in free will, but I had never considered that others would not.

"I've looked at this form," said a rotund man with a perpetual scowl. "It starts off with descriptions of sex acts and links to detailed drawings of your peoples' anatomy."

I gave him a moment to continue, but he didn't. "Yes, that's correct."

"So you admit it?"

Admit what? "We felt it was necessary to explain the expectations of brothel patrons as well as their possible anatomy to anyone interested in completing the form."

The beast comment woman leaned close to her camera. "*Children* are able to see that!"

"Perhaps," I said while resisting a shrug, "but we made certain to comply with local laws regarding access to those pages." I checked my notes. "They are only available after one enters their personal information, including their birth year, to place them at the age of consent."

"Local laws?" the woman sneered. "Local to where? Skid Row? The moon?"

The other two angry humans snickered with her.

"I believe by local," Alexandra Ocampo-Cruz said, "Administrator Rijal meant *American* laws. Confirming a viewer's age is what we require of the porn industry. Well, it's actually more than we require because they ask for—"

"Exactly!" the round man hollered. "Of all the things these aliens could've brought us and we get pornography."

I dragged my claws across the top of my head, grasping for calm. The humans had received medical technology that was making people weep with joy and relief the world over. They would soon have access to transportation technology that would allow them to travel outside of their own solar system. But no, they needed to focus on anatomical drawings. Even among a people who embraced open and available discussions of sex and sexuality, Norlons still did what we could to keep too much information from those too young to fully understand it. Those anatomy drawings were the same ones available to cubs of appropriate ages in their school books.

I let the humans talk to each other for a few moments more, heartened by the fact that the majority were defending the methods used to inform the volunteers. I knew that not all of them agreed with sex work, but they had the sense not to condemn those who saw nothing wrong with it. I could imagine there might be Norlons who disagreed with sex work in some way, but it was not a belief and they certainly didn't force it on anyone else.

"If I might share my own experiences," I said and ignored the lips that curled in disgust. "My mother paid for my first encounter when I was of age, and he was as instructive and gentle as anyone could want for their overeager and impatient son."

"*He?*" the man practically screeched. "Are you a homosexual tiger?"

Goddess give me strength. I bit back what I wanted to say and tried something else instead. "I am neither a tiger nor a homosexual. As I've said before, my people are Khess, and if I had to label my sexuality, I would use pansexual as I care not about the gender of my sexual partners."

One of the more reasonable men among them cleared his throat and said, "I think the point Administrator Rijal is making is that in Norlish culture such an event is normal and acceptable." He chuckled. "I'm pretty sure my first sexual partner would've appreciated it if I'd known more than I did."

"Gentle and instructive is wonderful," another woman added.

"Look," snapped a very polished man with a greasy smile. Everyone startled into silence at his volume, which I assumed had been his goal. "I'm not saying no American can participate. What I'm saying is that there's already a subsection of people who prostitute themselves. Why not just give them to the aliens?"

I stared in disbelief. I knew sex work happened in America, but also that it was deemed illegal and often done by those who felt they had no other method of earning money. Because it was unregulated, there was no dedicated medical care or even basic protections available to the workers. Disease, assault, and even murder was common. Drug abuse seemed to coincide as well. To suggest that we simply "take" those people—

Alexandra gasped in outrage. "Are you seriously suggesting that they take away the prostitutes? A section of the population that hasn't had a choice in the work they do? Why not give them the drug addicts, too?" she snapped.

"That's actually a good idea," the man said. "They're probably used to selling themselves for their next fix. It would help clean up a lot of neighborhoods for the good, Christian citizens of Indiana."

I nearly cut the connection, sharing the horror that several faces were conveying, but some small part of me that was meant to be a professional stopped me. After a deep breath, I said, "While we would happily assist those who feel they have no choices with finding another sort of work or other methods of improving their situations, we are actually seeking humans who are truly interested in providing and receiving pleasure with paying clients as a career."

"A career?" the woman scoffed.

Alexandra said, "In several other countries sex work is deemed a profession where the workers receive medical care and—"

"*Other* countries being the key phrase there, girlie."

"Don't you dare diminish my—"

"This is ridiculous! We're debating the wrong thing here—"

"Let's put this to a vote. All in favor of removing the undesirables from our states, say aye."

I saw red and muted them all again. As clearly as I could say it while my jaw was clenched, I said, "Thank you for your input regarding these matters, but we will proceed with selecting and interviewing the volunteers from the *two million* that we already have."

I ended the call and slumped back in my chair with a long sigh. The silence was a blessed relief, but it didn't last long, and I really should've known that it wouldn't.

"Should I book you in for a meeting with Prince Ye Lena to make your case for ignoring the leaders of this world and just doing whatever you want?"

I snorted and rubbed at my eyes, not bothering to look over at my assistant. Layleen, a gray and long-eared Pip, was a former brothel worker who'd happily left the business when she'd found her mate amongst her clients. She was currently pregnant with triplets and that hormonal situation had definitely impacted how freely she spoke to me.

"Yes, please," I said with a grin. "Let our illustrious leader know the many ways in which I've fucked this up and see if he has time to guide me through repairing everything. If you wouldn't mind."

"Absolutely, sir." She popped up from her chair and there was a definite hop in her step as she left the room.

I stayed where I was and sighed again. I should've become a bread maker like my father and left brothels and politics to some other fool.

My grandmother was probably cackling in the Great Beyond over how I was handling things. She'd been the one to leave me her brothel and instill her standards of stewardship in me. I saw myself as the leader of a people and took care of them in the best way I knew how. Bringing in new workers to fill a client need had seemed like the logical next step, so of course I'd answered the call to join the delegation to Earth.

"Idiot," I muttered to myself even as I approved the computer's request to upload the session. Yes, I was going to cause a few issues with this, but that wasn't new. Maybe if the delegation had come here asking for oranges instead of sex workers as the one thing they would like in return for their help, I would be seen as a hero.

Now that I knew what a devil was, I felt as though that title fit me much better anyway.

Get your copy of *Bound to the Tiger Scout* in ebook, paperback, or Kindle Unlimited via my website, delaneyrain.com.

ABOUT THE AUTHOR

Delaney Rain is an author of M/M paranormal romances featuring supernatural creatures and the men who love them.

Come for the GRR
Stay for the AWW

Read Chapters on Patreon
https://www.patreon.com/delaneyrain

ALSO BY DELANEY RAIN

FURRY ALIEN MATES

Knotted by the Wolf Prince

Claimed by the Fox Captain

Bound to the Tiger Scout

Captured by the Dragon Warrior

Hooked on the Otter Doctor

DELANEY'S SEA MONSTERS

The Sea Monster's Mate

Aquaculture Affair

DELANEY'S BIGFOOT

The Bigfoot's Mate

For Fur's Sake

Double Bigfoot Trouble

DELANEY'S INCUBI

The Incubus's Mate

Friends of the Incubus's Mate

DELANEY'S DEMONS

The Demon's Mate

A Death Worth Living

STANDALONES

Tentacles and Other Stocking Stuffers

The Demon's Dealbreaker

The Aliens' Mate

The Red Dragon's Mate

The Unicorn's Mate

The Minotaur's Mate

FEATURING PROWL'S *IS IT OUT THERE?* SHOW

The Red Dragon's Mate

The Demon's Mate

For Fur's Sake

Double Bigfoot Trouble

Printed in Great Britain
by Amazon